CLARET DREAMS

HISTORIC HICKORIES IN THE MODERN BRITISH OPEN

Tim Alpaugh

iUniverse, Inc.
New York   Bloomington

Claret Dreams
Historic Hickories in the Modern British Open

iUniverse books may be ordered through booksellers or by contacting:

iUniverse
1663 Liberty Drive
Bloomington, IN 47403
www.iuniverse.com
1-800-Authors (1-800-288-4677)

Because of the dynamic nature of the Internet, any Web addresses or links contained in this book may have changed since publication and may no longer be valid. The views expressed in this work are solely those of the author and do not necessarily reflect the views of the publisher, and the publisher hereby disclaims any responsibility for them.

ISBN: 978-1-4502-3524-2 (sc)
ISBN: 978-1-4502-3525-9 (dj)
ISBN: 978-1-4502-3526-6 (ebook)

Library of Congress Control Number: 2010908496

Printed in the United States of America

iUniverse rev. date: 06/16/2010

To Alexandra and Courtney

PREFACE

H ave you ever given any thought as to how Bobby Jones, Harry Vardon, or Walter Hagen would fare in a modern PGA event? Two thoughts come to my mind. If they could use today's modern equipment, would their ball striking skills separate them from today's players? Or, if they had to use the hickory-shafted creations that were state of the art in their era, how would the modern ball change their game? Could they compete? Could they win? There is no question that the developments in golf equipment have brought about longer shots, balls that spin and stop on a dime, and the ability for the average player to occasionally hit a shot that leaves him considering turning pro. But Bobby Jones would often hit a tee ball, with an old hickory, more than three hundred yards. Harry Vardon could chip over an opponent's ball and into the cup, from a stymied lie. The handmade clubs in the hands of the golfers of the "Golden Age" were like paint brushes in the hands of Picasso or Michelangelo.

And so I decided to allow this hypothetical game to take place. The historical details and events are, as they happened. The MacCoren family and their solitary set of Old Tom Morris golf clubs are the fictional vehicle by which we allow my theory to be tested. We travel back in time through the eyes of a weathered veteran caddie. We examine the history of golf. We acknowledge the men who shaped the game into the pastime we now enjoy. We note the evolution of the golf ball, the inception and development of the British Open, and experience that which we can only imagine in our "Claret Dreams".

I would like to thank my mother for both my presence and her support. To Mike Policano, thanks for your many suggestion and boundless enthusiasm. To those who have read and provided unbiased critical evaluations, I am forever in debt. And to Allan Robertson, Old Tom Morris, and the patriarchs of golf throughout Scotland in the 1860s, thank you for fostering a game that we have yet to perfect one and a half centuries later.

CHAPTER ONE

Slivers of dawn's light peek through the shutters of my den and dance across my eyelids. I awake to the realization that I will have the grand opportunity to enjoy yet another day of God's beneficence. After a few moments I stir slowly and extricate myself from an overstuffed and equally overused chair, that has for many nights become my bed. The chair, like a number of my possessions, reeks of pipe tobacco and the occasional whiskey spill. By all accounts my home is small, but it affords me all of the comforts I could ever ask for. My house, which some would call a cottage today, was built at the turn of the previous century by my father, a mason by trade, but a master of all skills. First occupied by him and his new bride, it has stood steadfast well past the length of their marriage. Despite the storms that raged both outside and in, it retains the same ruggedness and charm it had on their wedding day. The stone walls and hand-hewn beams bear testament to the craftsman's hand. The thatched roof was replaced with slate years ago after a careless fire nearly destroyed the dwelling. There is a small loft which houses some items I am attached to sentimentally, but for which I have little practical use. Built originally with two bedrooms, one was sacrificed as the modern conveniences of running water and septic gave birth to the often taken for granted, but truly appreciated, marvel of indoor-plumbing. The kitchen, too, is small but practical and the remaining space is an all-purpose den with a hearty stone fireplace that provides warmth to the entire house through the damp and chilly winters.

My favorite pipe, a meerschaum that was given to me by the golf pro at Troon on the occasion of my fiftieth year of service, rests in an ashtray. Its stained bowl, the head of and unknown sea captain, houses the charred remains of last night's tobacco. A trace of scotch lingers in the tumbler to its right. These two stalwart companions have helped me pass many an evening over the years.

I find myself, as I do most mornings, still wearing the clothes in which I began the previous day. I glance over through the doorway at my bed that again went unused. The bedding is drawn tight and the corners are crisp. Even though I've been a bachelor all my life, the simple act of making my bed has remained ingrained since my childhood. Not a day goes by that I don't think of my mother as I tuck the corners and push out the wrinkles. An even though the solace of my bed is truly enjoyable, the comforting, if not hypnotic, effects of single malt often prohibit me from escaping the embrace of my favorite chair as the evening draws to an end.

A few steps away is my kitchen and before too long a small pot of tea is left to steep. I pour myself a cup, with a bit of cream, and grab a scone that was fresh perhaps a day or even two before. It's not long before my aging bones find a seat on the porch. My rocker, which I fashioned by placing some curved barrel staves to an old kitchen chair, faces out to sea. The warmth of the morning sun takes the chill from the air and a fresh breeze off the water fills my lungs and reminds me how blessed I am to live here. I gaze out upon a view that may never grow old to me. It's a crisp and clear late summer morning here in the Ayshire coast of Scotland with the Isle of Arran in full view across the Firth of Clyde. As I do most days, I cannot help but to think back on a morning just like this in the late summer of 1962 and the Open Championship.

It is with unwavering amazement that the events of that week are indelibly etched in my memory. The usual names, the predictably unpredictable weather, and the whim of fate that catapults the most obscure player into the topic of conversation from afternoon tea to locker room banter in country clubs around the world. Such was the case with young Ian MacCoren. But before I get ahead of myself, I think it wise to go back and set the stage to what was, for me and many, perhaps the greatest human drama of the twentieth century.

CHAPTER TWO

The game of golf has many relatives but only one real matriarch. While there are claims to its ancestry from the Romans, the English, and the Dutch, the Scots first combined the efforts of a game involving a curved stick, a feather-stuffed ball, and a hole into the pastime we now know and enjoy as golf. While the evolution of the sport may have taken place over a number of centuries, the Scots take complete responsibility and full credit for having given birth to a game that has remained literally unchanged for nearly a quarter of a millennium. A written reference to the game of golf dates back as far as March of 1456 when Parliament, under King James II of Scotland, decreed the game of golf illegal as it interfered with much needed archery practice during a lengthy ongoing war with England. As a point of reference, Christopher Columbus was about five years old when the Scots were already smitten with the game of golf. Evolving as it has over the years, the basic premise is virtually the same. As lore would have it, golf was initially a way for shepherds to pass the lonely hours of wandering about, as their sheep grazed, by hitting a small stone with the end of a curved staff from place to place. During their trips they would often challenge themselves to reach a given target, like a rabbit hole, in fewer blows than they had done the day before. The land upon which they plied their newly found distraction was called "linksland".

Linkland is characterized by a stretch of land bordered by the sea that has remained unsuitable for farming. Wind, salt and erosion have left a meager layer of sand-based topsoil upon which a sturdy turf clings. The shepherds realized that a small stone hit properly across this tightly cropped turf would bounce and roll for quite some distance. Since time and nature had left the entire coastline of Scotland with land meeting this description, sheep had ample room to roam, and shepherds no shortage of playground upon which to maintain their sanity.

Over time, burrowing animals would clear away a small area to shelter themselves from the elements. As the wind blew in off the water it carried with it sand which would often deposit into these newly made holes. This gave birth to the bunker, as we know it today, and provided yet another obstacle for the shepherds in their daily distraction from the monotony of sheepherding. Over time, stones were replaced by wooden spheres and eventually by a ball known as a feathery.

Featheries were fashioned by artisans who used goose or chicken feathers, often as much as a top hat full, to make a single ball. The feathers were boiled in a huge pot of water, and while still moist, were stuffed into a small pouch consisting of three wetted pleats of cowhide or horsehide stitched together. Considerable strength and skill was involved as the volume of feathers often came close to, or exceeded, the hide's capacity. The pouch was then stitched closed and, as the leather dried and shrunk the feathers dried and expanded resulting in a very hard orb. The freshly minted ball was then shaped into a sphere to aid in its flight. To keep the feathery from absorbing moisture from the wet turf, a coating of white-pigmented paint was applied. This resulted in a ball firm enough to withstand the mighty blow of a club fashioned by strapping beech, holly or blackthorn to the end of an ash or hazel shaft.

As interest in the game grew, nobles would take advantage of their large tracks of land as venues for the new sport. Since equipment was essential to the game, the need for professionals to fashion clubs and balls was of paramount importance. Such was the chosen field of one Thomas Morris.

CHAPTER THREE

I n 1834, at the age of fourteen, Tom Morris's father decided it was
time for him to learn a trade. While thatching, carpentry and
masonry work were all quite respectable trades, Tom's father had
another discipline in mind. His father contracted with a ball maker
named Allan Robertson to employ Tom for a period of nine years, four
as an apprentice and the balance as a journeyman. Allan Robertson
was considered to be the most revered and talented golf professional
in all of Scotland. He excelled in every aspect of the game. In 1858 he
achieved the unthinkable when he recorded the first sub-eighty round
of golf at St. Andrews. He was often hired to fashion an occasional golf
club. But his true talent, the one Tom Morris sought to learn, was that
of ball maker, notably featheries. So labor intensive were featheries to
produce that their cost often exceeded that of a new golf club. While
clubs would break from time to time out of misuse or anger, featheries
were often the victim of mishits or lost in the high grasses. To have a
young apprentice who would increase his production, and income, for
the mere expense of lodging and meals, was of great benefit to Allan
Roberson. In Tom Morris, Allan Robertson found not only a talented
disciple but also a friendship that would last beyond the term of his
servitude.

As the 1840s arrived so did the first major technological advance
since the wooden ball brought about the evolution of the feathery. In

the distant land of Malaysia the sap of the palaquium gutta tree was being harvested. It was dried into leathery strips that were bundled and shipped back to the U.K. When the strips were boiled and softened they could be used as insulation and shipping material. In 1843 Dr. Robert Paterson, a professor of divinity at St. Andrews University, received a statue from the Orient packed in a container of gutta percha shavings. Noting their texture and resilience, he boiled the shavings down and fashioned shoe soles for his family members. His son, a student at the University, noticed that the soles showed very little wear after nearly two years of constant use. In 1845 he boiled some of the material and fashioned himself the first rubber-based golf ball. Though often disputed, it was this discovery that led to the development of the gutta percha ball, or "guttie" for short. Initially the ball would travel as if it had a mind of its own. However, after being hit a number of times it was discovered that nicks in the smooth surface of the ball improved its aerodynamic qualities. Gutties were soon produced and stamped with ridges and protruding dimples allowing them to travel greater distances than the feathery. Since twenty gutties could be produced in the time it took to make one feathery, and the cost of materials was one fourth as much, the game of golf was now more accessible to the golfer of less means. This development ushered in the first widespread increase in the number of golfers and transformed golf to a sport of the common man. Unless he was willing to accept the new technology, this development spelled disaster to Allan Robertson.

Allan Robertson was a purist at heart. He could have joined the crowd and produced the new longer flying balls, but he felt the trend would result in the obsolescence of courses and the advent of longer layouts and even longer rounds of golf. This very concern remains at the core of golf's greatest debate to this day.

Allan Robertson was so averse to the new technology, that he forbade his protégé Tom Morris from availing himself of its development. One afternoon, with a few holes remaining in his round with a club member, assistant professional Tom Morris ran out of his coveted supply of featheries. In order to complete his final holes, he was forced to borrow a guttie from his playing partner. Robertson passed Morris in an adjoining fairway and, noticing the act of blasphemy, fired Tom on the spot. Tom Morris, despite his efforts to explain his transgression, found himself among the ranks of the unemployed.

At the time, the town of Prestwick was forming its own golf club. The gentlemen members sought out Tom Morris to design, build, and maintain their new layout. Allan Robertson's one-man campaign was unable to halt the progress of technology, but his stubbornness did allow Tom Morris to begin a new chapter that would change the game of golf forever. Tom Morris, his wife and their son Young Tom left for Prestwick and a new life outside the confines of St. Andrews. It was at Prestwick that the two Tom Morrises would meet a young lad named Ian MacCoren.

CHAPTER FOUR

Ian MacCoren was not a child of privilege, but rather the son of a humble gardener. He grew up in the town of Prestwick in a small home with his sister and parents. They were, by all measures, poor. They did, however, have their health and a family bond that is rare today. Ian's paternal grandfather was an uneducated laborer in the foundries of Glasgow. He struggled all his life and died a miserable death at too early an age. Ian's father, scarred by an impoverished childhood and the early death of his own father, vowed to provide a better life for his wife and children. Ian's father's employer was a wealthy gentleman who lived on a sprawling estate just outside of town. He had inherited a large manor and a sizeable fortune. Jovial, despite having lost both his children to childhood disease, he was quite philanthropic. He had taken Ian under his wing and cared for him as if he were his own. He went as far as to enroll Ian at the prestigious Ayr Academy.

The Ayr Academy counted among its attendees the children of great privilege as well as a handful of lower class students able to afford the significant tuition. Ian's father insisted that his son make the best of his employer's benevolence and rise to a higher standard in life than he himself had achieved. It was at the Ayr Academy that Ian met and became great friends of Young Tommy Morris.

Like all parents, Tom Morris wanted more for his children than most parents of his generation possessed. His son was to have a formal education before entering the world. Young Tom was enrolled at the Ayr Academy and he and Ian found themselves bound initially by the mixed blessing of being, but in other's eyes, not belonging. Their bond was strengthened by a sport they would both take to quite readily.

On any given day, when Young Tom was not holding a book, his hands were firmly grasping a golf club. He respected his father's wishes to obtain an education, but his passion rested in the game that had provided notoriety to his father and a comfortable existence to his family. Young Tom's friend Ian was introduced to the game and smitten from the start. As the two lads grew, so did their games. Ian had a natural talent for ball striking, but Young Tom was a student of his new discipline. He learned what the clubs could do to the ball and how to utilize this knowledge to his advantage. It was the science of the game that would distance Young Tom from Ian, his peers, and the golf community at large.

CHAPTER FIVE

In 1860, shortly after the unexpected death of Old Tom Morris's mentor Allan Robertson, an effort was made to determine his successor to the title of "Scotland's Greatest Golfer". At the time, Old Tom Morris was at Prestwick and his club was chosen to host the decisive tournament. A belt, known as the Challenge Belt, fashioned from Moroccan leather and adorned with silver medallions was to be presented to the winner. The competition consisted of three rounds of stroke play over the twelve hole course at Prestwick. Since golf professionals could ill afford to miss the time necessary for match play, stroke play format was established and remains the format of Open competition to this day. Of the initial eight entrants drawn from all corners of Scotland, Willie Park of Musselburgh posted a score of 174 and captured the title. Since his score was considered to be within the ability of amateurs, the tournament was opened to all golfers the following year establishing it as an "open" event. This new competition became the incarnation of the British Open, as we now know it. That year and the ensuing year old Tom Morris captured the title. He and Willie Park would be victorious in all but one year through the end of 1867 when Tom's seventeen-year old son Young Tom would take over.

It was initially decided that the Challenge Belt would be retired when it was won three years in a row. Perhaps the competitors felt that so rare was this possibility that the belts longevity was guaranteed. However, in 1868 and 1869, Young Tom Morris took the title and walked away, literally, with the Belt following his third consecutive victory in 1870.

As 1871 arrived, the Scots, having no prize for which to compete, did not hold an Open Championship. Later that year, Musselburgh and St. Andrews, each contributing ten pounds toward a new silver trophy, joined Prestwick as hosts of the Open Championship. The Morrisses were such a dominant force in golf that no provision was made for the retirement of the new trophy in fear that it would find its final resting place on the Morris mantel along with the Challenge Belt.

Allan Robertson's death in 1860 brought about, not only the advent of the British Open, but the need to fill his position as greenskeeper at St. Andrews. It was a few years before a deal could be struck to lure Old Tom Morris from his position at Prestwick. It was the first time Old Tom had returned since the guttie episode. His attachment to the game and St. Andrews would keep him there until his death nearly fifty years later.

With his son's best friend leaving for St. Andrews, Ian's father found himself facing a difficult decision. Old Tom had recognized a budding talent in his son's classmate as well as a friendship that made Young Tom a bit more gregarious. Ian's father decided to move the family to St. Andrews to pursue his son's perceived potential. During the ensuing years Ian and his new friend Young Tom were quite inseparable. While Young Tom was clearly his father's disciple, Ian had developed a game, superior to many, but lacking in the tenacity of that of his best friend. While he competed in a number of Open Championships over the years, Ian never finished higher than fourteenth place. Ian and Young Tom often competed in friendly matches with each other. They would, from time to time, team as partners in a fourball against fellow golfers David Strath and a young American studying in Scotland by the name of Charles Blair Macdonald. Escaping the ravages of the Great Chicago

Fire, and subsequent depression, Charles Blair Macdonald traveled to Scotland to stay with relatives and study at St. Andrews. Macdonald relished his matches with Ian and Young Tom. He would often talk at length with Old Tom about the qualities found in great golf courses. Years later Charles Blair Macdonald would take his newly born passion for the game back to his native Chicago and, along with some other gentlemen of means, establish the United States Golf Association. He became instrumental in the development of golf in America and was considered the "Father of Golf Architecture" in the United States. The existence of golf in the United States, to no small extent, owes its heritage to Old Tom Morris.

CHAPTER SIX

On Thursday September 2, 1875, Old Tom Morris, his son and Ian were in North Berwick to participate in a golf competition. Following the competition, as was most often the case, a money match was held. Sponsored by wealthy benefactors, the Morrisses were to challenge the Park brothers to a thirty-six-hole contest. The victors shared in the purse with their sponsors. Late that afternoon, with only a few holes remaining in their match, Old Tom was notified, by telegram, that his son's wife was in grave condition resulting from complications involving the birth of their first child. A yacht was made available to the three men to cross the Firth of Forth on a seven-hour journey back to St. Andrews. It was not until the boat had reached shore that Young Tom was given the complete and heart wrenching news of the loss of his wife and stillborn son. Several months later, on Christmas morning, Old Tom Morris went upstairs to wake his eldest son, who had moved back home following the tragedy. As he entered his room, Old Tom discovered the lifeless body of his son. Ian, like many others, had believed that his death was a result of a broken heart. However, it was determined that a blood vessel in his right lung had burst, allowing Young Tom to be with his bride and unnamed child.

Ian was as close to Old Tom as his remaining sons Jimmy and Jack. He remained with him through the ensuing months attempting to assuage the grief of a loss so heartfelt. Ian had expected his friend

Young Tom to return the favor by being best man when he wed that summer. It was with a proud but heavy heart that Old Tom himself stood in his son's place. Shortly thereafter, Ian and his wife Sarah left St. Andrews to enter into her family's business. Their journey would take them to the Isle of Arran.

CHAPTER SEVEN

Off the southwestern coast of Scotland, a drive and a lofted iron away from the Isle of Islay, exists the Isle of Arran. A rocky coastline encircles the island. Inland it is blessed with a variety of terrains from vast areas of pasture, soaring evergreens and dozens of brooks and streams. With no shortage of incredible views in every direction, Arran has been home to the Glenfurloch Distillery, established in the early eighteenth century. Having run out of male heirs to continue the traditions handed down from his ancestors, Mungo Glenfurloch had decided to pass the reigns to his only daughter Sarah's new husband Ian.

Ian was an industrious, well-mannered individual who learned a great deal more about dealing with people of different levels of wealth and entitlement than perhaps he did in the classroom. His father taught him the value of hard work and the finer rewards of making a living rather than inheriting one. The combination of drive and determination coupled with the humility of manual labor would serve the life of a distiller well. Mungo was delighted with Ian's enthusiastic curiosity and tireless devotion to both his work and his new bride.

Ian and his new bride wasted little time in providing a grandson to the beaming Mungo. The first MacCoren born off the mainland was named William in deference to Sarah's older brother who died as a young child. Despite the long hours of backbreaking labor involved in his new vocation Ian was thrilled to begin a new stage in his life. From time to time, however, Ian's thoughts fell back upon Young Tom and the fickleness of life. Ian had remained in touch with Old Tom Morris, writing often and with great interest of his friend's well being. Old Tom shared, with great enthusiasm, the joy of William's birth. Ian thought how difficult it must have been for Old Tom to set his own sorrow aside as milestones in both his and other's lives took place.

Tom Morris took Ian up on his invitation and attended the christening of William. Later that week, as evening fell, Ian lamented over his desire to play golf again. While the long evenings allowed time for such a diversion, there remained one giant obstacle. The Isle of Arran, like many places throughout Scotland, was without a golf course. This was about to change.

CHAPTER EIGHT

A t the time, Old Tom Morris was the revered greenskeeper at his beloved St. Andrews. Over the years, St. Andrews had evolved into a course with twenty-two holes and only twelve greens played out and back along the Firth of Forth. As play evolved and the volume of golfers vying for a single hole blossomed, a solution was needed to reduce the congestion and provide for safer playing conditions. Initially a number of shorter holes were consolidated resulting in eighteen, a benchmark that has remained the standard to this day. To further reduce the congestion, the greens were widened and a cup was cut on each end. The outward nine, as it is now played had white flags, the inward nine was outfitted with red flags fashioned from the worn coats of the club's distinguished members. Among his many duties at St. Andrews was the cutting of the holes, the top dressing of fairways, tees, and greens, and irrigation. And so it was the next step in the evolution of his trade that someone with so broad an understanding of golf course maintenance would dabble in golf course design and construction.

Old Tom Morris would help in the development of a course at the Isle of Arran. Waiving his customary architectural fee of one pound, Old Tom joined Ian as they designed the new layout. A belief has long been held that no architect could eclipse the efforts of golf's original architect, "Mother Nature". What Old Tom Morris did, with the help of his young friend Ian, was to identify the holes that nature had left in the island's formation many, many years before. Just as he had done some years earlier at Prestwick, Old Tom found twelve wonderful holes that would serve as the island's new layout. Since there was little, if any, soil moved in revealing the dozen holes, the course was ready for play in no time.

CHAPTER NINE

William grew in leaps and bounds. A respectful well-mannered young man, William was the pride and joy of his grandfather Mungo. He had developed a great curiosity about life and his surroundings on the island. An enterprising young man, he would wander the high grasses of the golf course and sell the balls he found to the players for pocket change. As William grew older and reached the age when his father first met the Morrisses, he received a gift that was to play an integral part in the MacCoren family history. On a quiet and beautiful afternoon in the summer of 1889 Old Tom Morris returned to the Isle of Arran to play a round of golf on the course he helped discover.

He turned to young William and with a glint in his eye asked, "Would you give your father and me the pleasure of your company in a round of golf?"

William was astonished, but at the same time embarrassed, by the request.

"I would be honored, but unfortunately I have only a few clubs that my father has handed down to me."

Old Tom's smile widened immeasurably as he reached for a canvas bag sitting next to his luggage. "Then these will have to suffice laddie."

William opened the bag to discover a complete set of handmade irons as well as a driver, brassie, spoon and cleek. There were also a half dozen of the new gutta percha balls. Of the hundreds and perhaps thousands of clubs Old Tom had fashioned over the years, he found himself particularly proud of these. Old Tom explained that the last time he poured this much attention and effort into a set of clubs, was when he made a set similar to these for his late son, when he was William's age.

Old Tom held up the putter. It's head, like all the other clubs, bore the cleek mark T. MORRIS. He bent at the waist to be eye to eye with William and with a certain air of pride exclaimed, "I put a bit more effort in these William, since I know how much you love the game." William, as his father had taught him, extended his small hand and, making eye contact with this bearded legend of the game, expressed his gratitude for a gift that would, unbeknownst to him, have immeasurable longevity and profound impact on the MacCoren generations to come.

"I'll cherish them forever," he gushed, "I've never seen anything more beautiful."

Old Tom told William that he would grow into the putter, but altering its length would affect its balance. Ian, though he himself had a set of clubs from Old Tom, looked on with great interest and a pinch of jealousy.

Ian turned to William, "Why don't we give them a try?"

It didn't take much arm-twisting before they were off to the first tee. Old Tom was pleased to see the course in such fine shape. They let young William hit the first tee ball. He choked down on his new driver and gave it a swing. It was as if there was a magical quality to the clubs because the ball took off and the three just stared.

Ian broke the silence, "Well, I've never seen you hit a ball so pure William." William and Old Tom just smiled as the love affair with his new clubs had begun.

William held true to his promise and looked after his gift like a mother bear and her cubs. His father had shown him little tricks to maintain the tackiness of the grips as well as the importance of keeping the faces and shafts of the clubs clean. Such was William's fascination with his new possession that he asked his Dad to show him how to make clubs. His first several attempts were crude at best, but as time passed, he developed a skill that would provide him a small profit in later years as visitors to the island walked away with some of his handiwork. Old Tom Morris had heard of William's passion and sent him a plane and some whipping cord to encourage his new hobby.

Years passed and the distillery thrived. William had taken a series of jobs at the distillery after school to help out his father. He was particularly fond of the barrel makers. His talents with shaping wood and forging metal came in handy as passed through this phase of his apprenticeship. Yet even after a long day of work, William and his father found time to get in a trip or two around the now mature Arran links. William's game had developed at a terrific pace and he soon was giving strokes to his father in friendly matches.

William was enjoying the carefree life of a bachelor in the ensuing years. He moved up the ladder at the distillery, but was never afraid to get his hands dirty if a worker was off ill for the day. His passion for club making continued as well and he was often called upon to make or repair some of the clubs for the locals. All too often requests were made for clubs like the ones Old Tom had made. He simply stated, "There can never be a club made to match those of the master."

CHAPTER TEN

One morning in 1908 Ian walked into the distillery with his head in his hand. "Dad, what's the matter?"

"He's gone, our beloved Old Tom has passed away."

The two men held each other looking for words to express their sorrow. Ian looked to Old Tom as a father figure, and while William had spent little time with the man his father so revered, the clubs he received established a bond with enormous emotional ties. William and his father were about to journey to St. Andrews. The two men boarded a ferry to the mainland and then traveled by rail the two hundred kilometers to their destination. William was fascinated by the vastness of the rolling countryside. As the train rolled on into the night, he listened intently to tales, both old and new, from his father of the two Toms and the incredible bond that the three men shared.

Such was the sorrow throughout all of Great Britain that sufficient time was given for distant travelers to make their way to the service. Since Old Tom had outlived his entire family Ian was asked if he might say a few words at the church. He found it unusual at first that he was as distraught, if not more, over Old Tom's death than he was many years earlier when his own father passed on. Such was this inexplicable bond that golf had established and fostered over the years. Ian opened his comments by explaining how he had come to share in the lives of both Tom Morrisses, and how they would again be reunited. Ian spoke of the incredible gift Old Tom had left, not only to Scotland, but also to the game of golf itself. He explained how golf was a metaphor for life, and praised Old Tom for the gifts he received of honesty, integrity and patience that thrive within each lover of the game. In closing, he noted that, though removed from us in life, Tom Morris would never be separated from the game of golf. William could not help but think of the gift he himself had received from the hands of a man so revered and so loved that his passing brought a country to tears.

Following the service William and his father visited with relatives and friends, some of whom had never met William before. They took the opportunity to play several rounds on the course Ian and Young Tom called home nearly forty years earlier. William was deeply impressed by the character and charm of St. Andrews. Even though they were there for a sad occasion, like true Scots, they brought their clubs and celebrated Old Tom's life, as he would have wanted them to. While many had seen or even owned a club or two from Old Tom Morris, players marveled at the quality and condition of those in William's possession.

CHAPTER ELEVEN

Three days after the funeral, William and his father visited a local pub that Ian had frequented as a young man. As Ian went on about their match earlier that day he noticed that William's thoughts and eyes were elsewhere.

"William, is everything all right?" William did not even hear his father's question. There, across the room, was the most strikingly beautiful woman William had ever seen. Ian turned to see what his son was so fixated on. Ian recognized the look, as it was the same blank stare he found on his face when he first saw his wife Sarah. Ian was convinced that William was a confirmed bachelor and that an heir to the distillery would have to come from one of William's sister's children. Ian was about to encourage William to say hello when William bolted from his seat and crossed the room.

William was a tall thirty-three year old man brimming with confidence and good looks. He was pursued by a number of women back in Arran, but he graciously rebuffed their advances. This was the first time he became the pursuer.

He approached the statuesque brunette and without an ounce of hesitation extended his hand, "Hi, I'm Will MacCoren, at the risk of sounding foolish I have to tell you that you're the most beautiful woman I've ever seen,"

Taken aback by this forwardness, but all the while blushing from his compliment, Claire Reilly extended her hand, "I'm Claire, Claire Reilly, it's a pleasure to meet you."

William was on cloud nine. Claire was nearly as tall as William, and when she stood to say hello his knees softened. Though ten years his junior, she possessed a maturity and sophistication of women much older than herself. If golf were not enough of a gift to receive from his parents, William was also blessed with a poise and insouciant charm few could match.

Claire was waiting to meet a few friends, but when they arrived she excused herself momentarily to inform them that she was otherwise engaged. When her friends saw William they smiled an assuring nod of approval and understanding.

As the contents and patrons of the tavern all but disappeared, William found himself captivated by Claire's every word. Conversation flowed easily when all of a sudden William realized he had forgotten his father. When he turned to look, Ian had paid his tab and was tipping his cap to William as he turned to leave. "I'll see you at the hotel," he mouthed as he smiled, a smile of reassuring acceptance.

In what seemed like the blink of an eye, the evening had passed. William and his new friend rose to head home.

Once outside William turned to Claire and asked, "May I have the pleasure of seeing you again?"

Claire was delighted by his request and wrote her address on a small note. She folded it and their hands touched as she passed it to him with a smile. William waved as she left in a coach for home. His feet hardly touched the ground as he made his way to the hotel.

Ian was still awake when William entered the room, "Well, how did it go?"

"Dad, I've never felt this feeling before. I think I'm in love."

William asked his father if he could stay back when the week was over. While Ian could use William back at the distillery, he knew the opportunity facing his son may not surface again and agreed. Saturday morning rolled around and William bid his father farewell, "I'll be home in a week or two Dad. I need to see where this is going."

"Don't rush love son, I'll see you when I see you."

On the third week anniversary of Ian's departure, William and his new bride-to-be returned to Arran. Ian and Sarah welcomed Claire to their family and wedding plans were undertaken. Claire was the eldest of five girls. Though her father was sad to see his first child leave the nest, he and his wife were both taken by William's charm and ambition, not to mention the overwhelming happiness they saw in their daughter's eyes.

After a brief honeymoon in Ireland to see relatives who were unable to make the wedding, William and Claire settled down in the small house William had built some years earlier. With each passing year Ian and Sarah were blessed with another granddaughter. Then, after three girls, a grandson arrived. Robert Morris MacCoren entered the world in the spring of 1912.

Ian turned to William and said, "Now you've got someone to pass those clubs on to."

CHAPTER TWELVE

The girls and their mother found countless ways to pass each day. They learned the art of making lace, quilting and other skills that would serve them as years passed. Although women played golf at the time, William limited his attention to Robert. Robert was all of about four when William fashioned him a set of clubs that was nothing shy of a miniature reproduction of those he received from Old Tom Morris. His young son took a shine to the new implements, but before too long he had outgrown their short shafts. A second set would follow, as Robert, much like his father, was a tall child. The art of club making was therapeutic for William and he derived a great deal of joy from both the process and the elation of the recipient.

Time passed quickly and before long it was Robert's twelfth birthday. With Ian looking on, William presented Old Tom Morris's clubs to his son. Just as with his father before him, Robert's game took on a mystical quality. William had fashioned a set of clubs, similar to those he had given to his son, so that he could join Robert on the links. Like true Scots, The MacCorens enjoyed camaraderie as much as the competitive rivalry. Each hole was contested against both par and the opponent, but only the accomplished shots and displays of talent and imagination were discussed after any round. Robert loved his grandfather very much. He sat for hours listening to tales of Young and Old Tom Morris. He knew all too well the history of Scottish golf and felt honored that someone so close to him on the MacCoren family tree had shared the company of golf "royalty".

Along the same time as Robert's game was evolving, a young lad by the name of Stuart Wallace was being introduced to the game. Stuart's father was an employee of the distillery. Like William, he passed on the traditions of the game to his son. Stuart was a natural and Robert often found himself frustrated by his inability to defeat his friend on the links. The rivalry improved Robert's game and brought the two friends closer. As adolescence evolved into adulthood, Robert and Stuart took on increasing responsibilities at the distillery. It took very little time before the two men were running the operations, splitting their skills into the various aspects of production.

In 1934, at the age of eight-eight, Ian passed away quietly in his sleep. His wife Sarah had passed away some years before, and Ian's zest for life had diminished greatly. The distillery was closed the day of the funeral. Most of the island was present to honor the man who provided not only a livelihood for the people of Arran, but a golf course on which to enjoy their leisure time for decades to come. A small bronze plaque was installed on the first tee box of the golf course recognizing Ian's relationship, and collaboration with Old Tom Morris. To those who play the course today, many will recognize the name of Old Tom Morris. However, if not for Ian MacCoren, the island of Arran would just be home to a great distillery.

William was approaching his mid fifties when he decided that Robert should take over the control of the distillery. He was still spry but he wanted his son to assume the mantle. At the end of the 1920s, as word spread about the twelve-hole layout, tourism to the island increased. Visitors would come over for the day, play golf, tour the distillery and return by nightfall filled with tales of great golf and often a bit of the island's finest single malt. A small clubhouse was built to welcome the players and process their greens fees. So profitable was the course from tourist's play that the locals played for free. The revenue provided for a full time greenskeeper and the equipment necessary to maintain the course.

Above the small fireplace at the clubhouse was a picture of Old Tom Morris hitting the inaugural shot on the opening day. In a shadow box was a replica of the putter he used that day as well as an old feathery he donated. Every visitor to the course marveled at the legendary equipment. William decided that he would spend his retirement working at the clubhouse and selling his hand-made clubs as souvenirs. He remained in the picture at the distillery as a consultant, but day–to-day decisions were now the domain of his son. Robert's best friend Stuart joined him in managing the production. While Robert considered Stuart an equal in the management of the distillery, William reminded him that family and tradition would have to take precedence.

Robert found little time for anything but work and golf, golf and work. He did, however, have the time to meet and fall in love with a beautiful young woman named Marie. Marie grew up on the island. She was a thoughtful and caring young woman who was blessed with a terrific sense of humor. Her father had worked at the distillery and often golfed with William over the years. It was through this connection that she and Robert came to be introduced. Marie was no stranger to the game of golf, having played nearly as long as her soon to be husband. She enjoyed spending time on the course with Robert in the early evenings. Marie's golf was purely social, but she could play well enough not to embarrass herself. An occasional birdie showed her medal and kept her interest in the game alive. Robert never thought he would find someone who could understand his obsession with both work and golf, but in Marie he did.

As the year 1940 approached, Robert and his new bride settled down in a small home Robert and William had built not far from William and Claire's home. The line of MacCoren golfers was about to be extended.

CHAPTER THIRTEEN

In the late summer of 1940 young Ian MacCoren was born. Named after his great-grandfather, Ian was the pride and joy of both Robert and his grandfather William.

Marie, however, suffered from complications that plagued the late pregnancy and delivery. The doctor reassured her that she would be fine, but she and Robert were saddened to discover that she could no longer have any more children. The couple decided to embrace the good news and not dwell on that over which they had no control. The future looked bright for the young couple when rumblings of social and political unrest began to take place throughout Western Europe.

As the War spread throughout Europe in the early 1940s a number of men from the island were called to active duty. Throughout Great Britain every able-bodied man over the age of eighteen was required to join the war effort. There were, however, circumstances where allowances were extended. Such was the case for Robert and his friend Stuart. They were contacted, along with other businesses, to continue production such that the troops would remain supplied. Robert was asked if he could reconfigure his operations to bottle water for the aid stations along the front. While he and Stuart were more than eager to get in and fight with their fellow countrymen, they felt a certain sense of patriotism with the duty thrust upon them.

Whiskey had always been bottled in small manageable amounts, which corresponded to the batches that were distilled. The volume of bottling required by the war department would mean that production would increase ten fold. A number of women, whose husbands were involved in the war effort, provided a substantial portion of the labor force. William put aside his club making practice and pitched in from time to time where he could. The equipment was converted to fill the bottles with pure, clean well water from a source nearby the distillery. Each morning, a new supply of bottles would arrive at the docks. The previous day's production would be loaded on board and the process repeated. Robert and Stuart were instrumental in both the conversion of the plant and its successful operation.

As World War II came to a close, men were returning home to cheers of enthusiastic islanders. Some of Robert's friends, however, did not return. A great period of exuberance coupled with solemn remembrance followed the conclusion of the war. Part of the celebration that was taking place all throughout Great Britain involved the imbibing of whiskey. With supplies of whiskey dwindling over the years, there became a pressing need to return the distillery to the production of something with a little more kick than water.

CHAPTER FOURTEEN

Robert and Stuart were scheduled to begin the reconfiguration of the bottling operations that fateful Saturday. Stuart was unable to make it to work because of a stomach virus that had plagued a number of workers. Robert felt confident he would be able to make the necessary alterations by himself. One of the gears that drove the belt feeding the bottles became erratic. As Robert stretched for the shut-off switch he lost his balance. As he reached to brace his fall his hands fell squarely on the malfunctioning gear. As if in slow motion, Robert watched in horror as his hands were crushed by the equipment. A blood-curdling cry drew the attention of a young worker who rushed to his aid. As blood poured from his hands the worker applied make shift tourniquets. Robert turned an ashen grey as he was carried to a nearby truck and rushed to the island's physician.

The morphine that was administered helped Robert sleep through the night. Marie and William were by his bedside as he awoke the following morning. His hands were encased in bandages but he could see that they were not complete. He tried to keep from crying as the doctor told him they were unable to repair the damage. Four of Robert's fingers were completely removed and three others were lost at the first joint. William and Marie tried to no avail to assuage his profound despair with regard to his condition.

Robert was so despondent in the days following the accident that

Marie thought he might take his own life. Feeling incomplete and at an arms length away from the constant reminder of his unalterable condition, Robert openly questioned his purpose in the world.

Marie looked him squarely in the eyes and asked, "Do you want your son Ian to grow up without a father?"

This sobering thought put Robert's life and condition into perspective and he began to cry. So blessed were the MacCorens, that this was truly the first tragedy to befall them in decades. Since the birth of his son, Robert's life had taken on a special purpose. He was not about to let this setback negatively affect the course of Ian's life. He vowed to Marie that he would not do anything foolish and he thanked her for opening his eyes to what really mattered in life.

Time went by quickly and, with Marie and William's support, Robert's hands and mind healed. Ian was growing in leaps and bounds. Robert knew it would not be long before his son was ready to tackle his first round of golf. Ian had developed into quite a good putter using a new shortened mid-shafted creation of his grandfather. William was incredibly saddened by the accident, wondering often about the lost potential his son possessed and the emotional toll his accident had taken. He and Robert poured their attention and collective golf knowledge into their new disciple.

In no time, the day arrived to celebrate Ian's twelfth birthday. A great gathering of family and close friends made for a joyous occasion. Robert's good friend Stuart returned to Arran for the celebration. Not long after the accident, and feeling a considerable amount of guilt, Stuart left for the mainland. While Stuart apologized numerous times for his absence that day, Robert would have none of it. Robert tried to convince his best friend that his accident was simply that, an act of fate.

Stuart left the following morning imploring Robert and William to visit one day. He told William that his skills as a club maker would be quite profitable on the mainland. They were gracious about the invitation but each knew he would probably never leave. Robert was very busy with the day-to-day operations of the distillery, and William was spending more and more time caring for his wife. Claire's health had slowly diminished in the previous year. Since the doctors had little understanding of cancer at the time, they attributed her condition to menopause. William was concerned, but Claire insisted that he not worry.

Shortly after Stuart's departure Robert called his son to the den for a little talk. When Ian entered the room he saw his father and grandfather sitting at the couch with a bag of golf clubs. After the accident Robert had put the clubs away for protection and to help diminish the disappointment of not being able to use them. Ian had never seen the clubs before but they bore a striking similarity to the ones his grandfather played with and made.

Robert smiled at Ian as his son took a seat. William and Robert had not told Ian of the tradition of passing Old Tom Morris's clubs down, and they were bursting with the anticipation of Ian's response. Without any further delay Robert passed the clubs, bag and all, to Ian. Robert's eyes were damp with tears as he told Ian that he had looked forward to this day since Ian's birth. Ian took the clubs out of the bag, one at a time, examining them with great intent. He sat starry eyed as his father and grandfather told him of the club's heritage. William told Ian that his love of the game blossomed the day Old Tom handed him this treasure.

Ian hugged his father and said, "I promise to honor this gift all my life. This is the best present a kid could ever get."

Robert and William shared Ian's sentiment, as they both recalled the day they were blessed with this same act of generosity and trust.

Robert broke the silence by saying, "Well let's see if they still work."

The three caretakers headed out to the course to breathe some new life into this cherished treasure. Ian had developed quite a swing with the clubs William had fashioned for him over the years. Robert and William stood together as Ian addressed the ball. He stood back and looked at his father, who grinned from ear to ear. He then turned to William. William winked as a grin flashed across his weathered face. Ian drew the club back for the first time. The magic was still there. The ball flew down the first fairway as all three smiled an appreciative grin.

Ian and his clubs were inseparable over the ensuing years. With each passing year, Ian's mastery of the game improved. At fourteen he had established a junior mark for the course. He would go on to lower that score more than half a dozen times before his eighteenth birthday. William and Robert spent endless hours, on and off the course, teaching Ian the many facets of the game. Though Robert could no longer demonstrate to Ian the shots he would require to master the game, he hammered home the mental side of golf. Ian flourished on the links. He absorbed every ounce of guidance his two teachers would offer.

William and Robert knew there was more to the game than the physical and mental acumen. Sportsmanship, honesty, and integrity are the building blocks upon which the game, and for that matter, life is built. All the swing thoughts, skills, and talent in the world fall short when honor is not respected.

William summoned Ian to his side one afternoon and imparted his greatest advice. "When the game of golf becomes more than that, a game, and the joy and passion is gone, put down the clubs and walk away." Ian wondered what could ever make the game of golf anything less than enjoyable.

CHAPTER FIFTEEN

As he reached his mid seventies, William was considering both his own mortality and his usefulness at the distillery. He was growing more and more anxious each passing day. He lived alone after his wife Claire passed and his behavior was often a concern for Robert and Marie. Though he was always invited to functions held by his extended family, he often felt it was out of obligation that his presence was requested. Robert and Marie were always gracious, as was Ian, but there always came a pregnant pause at the end of the day when he would wander home alone.

One evening at dusk Ian watched as the solitary silhouette of his grandfather disappeared into the sunset by the cliffs overlooking the port. No body was ever found, but it was believed that the sea had taken William. Perhaps his wife's passing or the guilt he housed following Robert's accident brought him to leap to his death. Everyone believed that Ian's birth and the ever-increasing demand for his golf clubs had brought about a renewed outlook in William. Despite not having found a body, a funeral was held and nearly the entire population of this small but close-knit island was in attendance.

Robert and Ian spent many quiet evenings walking the course.

A breeze blew in off the ocean as Robert smiled, "He's still out there in the tall grass and the many bunkers."

Ian missed his grandfather a great deal and felt it was up to him to honor his memory by capitalizing on the knowledge he had imparted and becoming the best golfer he could become. Ian developed great skills as the years passed. He was not only a fine golfer but a gentleman as well. Robert took great pride in hearing praise of Ian's game but even greater pride in the statements acknowledging him as a fine gentleman. While Robert could not demonstrate with great dexterity the many shots that would be needed from time to time to deal with the whims of nature, his words proved more valuable than any instructional guide.

The twelve holes routed out by his great grandfather and Old Tom Morris held very little challenge for Ian as he reached the end of his teen years. While there were visitors to the island who tested their skills on the course, few came close to Ian's mastery and no one could ever beat him. With little to challenge his golf talents Ian was growing bored.

CHAPTER SIXTEEN

The summer of 1962 had arrived and Ian, now a mature twenty-two year old, had asked his father if he might be able to attend The Open Championship at nearby Troon. Ian, like every young golfer of his day, had fantasized that his final putt on any given round was to capture the Open Championship. To see his idols at such a prestigious event first hand was a dream come true. Robert's dear friend Stuart lived nearby and was all too happy to host his friend's only son.

Ian had never left the island, though he had heard tale from both William and Robert of the incredible courses that hugged the coast and dotted the countryside of Scotland, England, and Ireland. To bear witness to the world's greatest golfers on the historic Troon would be an incredible treat.

A twenty-mile ferry to the mainland and a brief train ride south along the coast would bring Ian to his destination. His country seemed so incredibly large. The landscape was dotted with many courses, but he found himself hard pressed to spot any with the natural beauty and variety of his own.

As the train arrived at the station Uncle Stuart was waiting. It wasn't difficult to recognize Ian, as he was now the spitting image of his father. Stuart was not Ian's uncle by relation but was always referred to as such as Ian grew up. Stuart waived to Ian bellowing out his name. He was a taller, handsomer version of the lad had last seen at William's funeral.

Stuart gabbed Ian's satchel and clubs, "Is this it?"

"This is all I hold dear to me Uncle Stuart," Said Ian.

"Stuart will suffice Ian, you're a man now."

Stuart smiled, "Oh I remember these clubs. They were your father's pride and joy." A quiet pause came over the two as they both reflected on the accident and what might have been.

"How's your father doing Ian?" Stuart inquired, "It's been quite a number of years."

Ian paused for a moment, thinking of his grandfather, "After Granddad passed away, he's taken a different view of life. He seems to be enjoying his leisure time much more than before. Mom and I have even seen him smiling now and again at the most unusual circumstances. He's no longer bitter about the accident though I'm sure he thinks about it all too often."

Stuart was eager to show Ian the sights, "Well I've got a big agenda for us this week lad. There's still a lot of daylight, so let's settle in and see if we can't play a few holes this evening."

Stuart was a single man of some means after his father passed and left him a tidy inheritance. Though he didn't make a big fuss about it, he was recognized by the townspeople for his generosity and philanthropic deeds. His favorite tavern was on the way home and they always served a hot meal.

Stuart returned to the table and passed Ian a pint, "You're plenty old enough to enjoy a pint my friend. To adventure." Little could Stuart comprehend the prophecy of such a comment.

They had a quick meal and were catching up on island happenings when Stuart said, "Enough small talk, lets drop off your kit and get to the golf course."

Not far from the tavern was Stuart's house, a modest home by most standards, but more than adequate for this bachelor's carefree life. Ian had heard his father's congratulatory praise over his friend Stuart's inheritance and good fortune. He was surprised, but at the same time impressed, with these humble surroundings. Ian settled in quickly, all too anxious to experience golf outside of Arran.

Not far from Troon was a challenging layout that at one time had been the site of an Open qualifier. Stuart was no stranger there and was welcomed with open arms.

"Bobby," said Stuart, "This strapping lad is Ian MacCoren, my best friend's son."

Bobby extended his hand, "Welcome Ian, any friend of Stuarts is more than welcome here."

Stuart and Ian grabbed their clubs and wandered the short distance to the first tee.

Stuart stood back at the first tee giving Ian the honors, "Let's see if Old Tom's clubs work as well for you as they did for your father." With little hesitation, Ian withdrew his driver and in a most fluid demonstration of power and balance sent his tee shot down the first fairway. Stuart stood there in absolute silence.

"Is everything okay?" asked Ian.

Stuart stood a little slack jawed, "Your father was right when he said I wasn't ready to witness such a beautiful sight." Stuart had developed a terrific game as a youth on Arran and in the ensuing years, but he stood in absolute awe of Ian's effortless distance and control. There was a fair breeze blowing that evening and Stuart was interested in seeing how Ian handled the elements. Left to right, right to left, low running shots and distance control. Ian had a mastery of the game that exceeded Stuart's wildest imagination. Oh, and Ian could putt. He took only a couple of holes before he had mastered the speed and before long looked as though he had grown up on this course.

"Well, I used to have the course record Bobby," said Stuart, as he and Ian entered the pro shop. "I just witnessed perhaps the finest display of golf skills I've ever seen."

Bobby had a bit of news for Stuart and Ian, "Well Stuart, I just received a call from the tournament office. One of the American lads was in a car accident, nothing serious, but there's another spot in tomorrow's qualifier. I was going to offer it to you, but perhaps young Ian might be interested."

All this was a bit too much for Ian to digest. He had traveled from home to be a spectator, but a twist of fate had placed him one step, albeit a large one, away from competing in one of golf's most historic and revered competitions.

CHAPTER SEVENTEEN

Despite Stuart's insistence that Ian get some rest that evening, Ian was like a child on the eve of Christmas. He dozed off from time to time only to wake to the realization that this reality was, in fact, a dream come true. Stuart entered Ian's room the following morning only to find Ian dressed and sitting at the foot of the bed.

"Do you think you can bring yourself to eat something?" Ian nibbled on toast and eggs but his thoughts were elsewhere. Should he call his father or would that add even greater turmoil to the cauldron bubbling away in his stomach. Stuart's advice was to wait and see what the day brought. They collected their belongings and headed out to the course.

As they arrived at the course, Ian looked about to absorb all that he could. The course bore a striking similarity to the one he and Stuart played the evening before. Although the course was unlike the links of Arran, the air permeated with the same smell of heather and freshly cut grass. Dew blanketed the fairways as a cool air lingered from the short evening. Maintenance crews scurried to address finishing touches to what, for many, was about to be the most physically and mentally exhausting day of their lives. As was the case for all British Opens until the late sixties, all players, regardless of their achievements or notoriety, had to make their way into The Open by means of a thirty-six-hole qualifier. A number of proven veterans were there with a certain air of confidence but a lingering doubt from the memories of previous attempts. Others knew they were outmatched but they were sticking it out with the belief in miracles that today everything might click and their lofty dreams would be fulfilled.

Ian gathered his clubs and with Stuart by his side made his way to the registration table. A number of local players and club officials recognized Stuart and made their way over to greet him.

An acquaintance of Stuarts was standing near the registration table as the two arrived, "Times are so hard now Stuart that you've had to take up caddying?"

"On the contrary, this is my friend's son, Ian MacCoren. He's a late entry but my money is on him today."

To a man, those who passed as Ian got settled in at the practice range looked at his clubs. Many had only seen wooden shafted clubs on the walls of their home course clubhouses. Fewer still had seen them in use, much less in an event as important as this one.

As relaxed as Ian was with a golf club in his hands, he found himself noticeably nervous and uncertain of the day's unfolding events. Unable to relax and with tension in his hands and arms, Ian took his first swing at the practice range. The clubface nearly missed the ball and it fluttered quickly to the right.

"My money's on him today," one of Stuart's acquaintances chided as he walked away to practice his putting.

"It's not too late to get a real set of irons son," said one of the veterans in a rather condescending manner. Ian politely smiled and rolled another ball into position. This one didn't even go as far as the first. Well a lot of heads shook from side to side and eyes rolled as Ian's heart sank deep in his chest. Nerves were often as taut as a snare drum and Ian was not the only one showing their effect. Many a player dealt with his demons in their own way. More than one breakfast was left behind a bush that morning.

Stuart stepped forward and placed Ian's hands in his.

"Ian you have more game than the lot of them put together. Close your eyes and take yourself far away from here for a moment. Put yourself on the first tee at Arran." Ian's breathing had noticeably slowed and his hands relaxed. Stuart released Ian's hands and stepped back. Ian opened his eyes and saw only the ball. The air was silent as he drew back his club. The silence was broken by the crisp sound of the ball and wooden clubface making contact. This sound was unlike any that the other golfers were accustomed to hearing. Heads were now turned back as the other players traced the ball's flight through the clear blue morning sky. Pure, thought Stuart, Ian is back. Stuart smiled at Ian and the corners of Ian's mouth curled up ever so slightly as he nodded in appreciation.

"Play your game Ian, the rest will take care of itself."

Ian and Stuart strode to the first tee and exchanged pleasantries with Ian's playing companion and his caddy.

A tall strapping gentleman extended his weathered right hand, "Timothy McGarry, pleasure to meet you."

Ian had not heard of McGarry before, but had he known he was a former two-time Irish Open champion his nerves would no doubt have been pushed to their limit. Stuart did not think it necessary to burden Ian with McGarry's accomplishments as he too smiled and shook hands. McGarry looked at Ian's clubs the way someone looks at the scars from a bad burn. He was more than curious but felt uncomfortable staring. He too had only seen clubs like Ian's on the wall of his home course back in Portmarnock. That someone would attempt to use them given the changes in technology was beyond him.

McGarry had honors as they began their round. Whatever butterflies circled about Ian's stomach had all been erased. Ian teed his ball and sent a high draw down the right side of the fairway in the silence of the morning air. Ian turned to Stuart and the two smiled as they began their quest for a spot in the Open Championship. McGarry had always been recognized as a long hitter, but when Ian's ball flew by his before landing he became a little more curious about these ancient implements.

"He can drive it all right," said McGarry to his caddy, approaching his own drive and unaccustomed to hitting first, "But there's more to this game than just that." Stuart might have recognized the look on McGarry's face as Ian's second shot fought a left to right wind and released across the green, settling just two feet from the pin. It was the same look of incredulity he bore the day before seeing Ian execute one shot after another with a control few have ever witnessed before. Ian swallowed hard as he stood over his putt.

Stuart placed his hand on Ian's shoulder, "Step away Ian."

Ian stood back and Stuart whispered in his ear. "You can make this one in your sleep lad, the hard work is behind you." Ian regrouped and confidently tapped the putt in for birdie. Both Stuart and Ian shared a huge sigh of relief as they made their way to the second tee. Having not seen the course before Ian relied entirely on Stuart's experience and local knowledge.

Stuart passed Ian his club, "Take a mighty swing, there's wind up there we can't feel." Ian felt he had too much club but he trusted Stuart's counsel. As the ball soared high above the green, the two appeared a bit concerned about the club selection. Then, as if a parachute were deployed, Ian's ball fell quietly down to the green settling about eleven feet below the pin.

"There's about four inches of borrow from the left," said Stuart. "Speed is everything lad, don't be shy." Ian chose his line and struck his putt boldly. It rode into the cup as if on rails and as quickly as that, Ian was two under par after as many holes. Neither Stuart nor Ian wanted to pinch himself and awaken from this blissful dream. Much the same happened on the third and fifth holes and after an eagle chip-in on the sixth, Ian stood at six under par on a course that had embarrassed the world's greatest that morning. Word spread quickly and before too long the gallery following Ian and McGarry had swelled to nearly two hundred curious spectators. All the attention was quite familiar to McGarry, but Ian had never played before more than a handful. The attention and perhaps the gravity of his accomplishments had caught up with Ian as he proceeded to bogey both seven and eight.

"Let's right this ship before we find ourselves as spectators and not participants," said Stuart. Ian collected himself and hit a mashie two hundred and eighteen yards to within a foot of the hole. The gallery, that had grown respectfully quiet, erupted and Stuart and Ian knew they were back on track.

Ian continued to play as if he were the only one on the course as birdies fell on eleven, thirteen, and fourteen. Questions arose about the course and Open record. "Sixty-five by the great Bobby Locke, back in 1958," said on of the spectators following the pairing. Stuart was about to witness a piece of history. He held onto Ian's ear for the remainder of the round calming him and controlling his nerves. As the final putt fell on eighteen, Ian had not only set his second course record in as many days, but he was half way to qualifying for The Open.

As first round scores were posted and the players grabbed a quick bite between rounds, some players withdrew with little chance of a comeback while others began to strategize on their remaining eighteen. Some players congratulated the unknown rookie while others, who recognized the importance of what lied ahead, focused solely on themselves. Arnold Palmer and Gary Player, who had developed a great friendship over the recent years of competition, had graciously sought out Ian and, in a true display of sportsmanship, congratulated the youngster on his accomplishment. They wished him luck in the afternoon round and said they hoped to see him at The Open.

Ian was practically giddy with excitement, "Can you believe that? Arnold Palmer and Gary Player congratulated me."

"Ian," said Stuart, "You have the game to compete with them. Don't get all star struck or they will see you at The Open, but from the gallery."

The afternoon round had the same pairings as the initial round, with the exception of a few withdrawals. Ian again greeted Timothy McGarry at the first tee but this time McGarry was a bit less cavalier.

Stuart passed Ian his driver on the first tee, "It's time to again focus your thoughts on the game at hand." Despite Ian's youth he had an incredible ability to focus his thoughts and energies on a specific task while virtually shutting out the rest of the world. Robert had explained to Ian how he would focus so intently on his infant son that the excruciating pain of his accident all by disappeared. Ian was able to channel his thoughts in the same manner, often not even recalling the goings on around him.

The second round started much like the first and a gallery that had swelled to nearly four hundred began to wonder if they might bear witness to another blistering round. Having now played the course, Ian was now a bit more comfortable with what lie ahead. Stuart began to get a bit excited himself as the round wore on and Ian had to pull him aside.

"Stuart," said Ian, "I know this is incredibly important, but remember it's really still just a game." Just a game thought Stuart, no it's for the British bloody Open for crying out loud. Ian's carefree demeanor seemed to calm Stuart as they continued their quest. While a few putts failed to fall Ian's game was spot on and he ended the day with a sixty-nine and a total of one thirty-three. This was good enough for titleist honors. Ian was going to play in the British Open.

The Open, as it is referred to in Great Britain, is considered to be the greatest of all golf competitions. Dating back to 1860 it predates the other three majors by a combined total of over one hundred years. After the retirement of the Championship Belt, and the decision to share the cost of the new trophy and venue, the Open Championship resumed in 1872. That year it was again won by Young Tom Morris and his name is perhaps the first that a new champion looks for aside from his own. It was decided in 1871 that Prestwick, St. Andrews and Musselburgh would contribute equally to the purse and the Open would be rotated between the three layouts. The three clubs also got together and commissioned a new trophy to be presented to the winner. In true Scottish fashion, they decided that the prize would not be retired regardless of the number of victories in a row a player had amassed. At the time, members of clubs paid fines or bets with a Bordeaux or Claret as their form of currency. The golfers would bring their wager to the club in a pitcher or decanter and partake in the spoils of the victor following the match.

To this end, it was decided that a silver wine vessel would be commissioned as the esteemed reward for the ensuing Open Championships. It received its reputation as the "Claret Jug" in this manner. The claret jug has long been the symbol of golf's greatest achievement. The thought of having his named carved along with those of Harry Vardon and Bobby Jones was a bit too much for Ian to digest.

Pats on the back, hand shakes and applause followed Ian and Stuart that evening. Stuart phoned Robert when they returned home that night. Ian thought he would burst with excitement. Robert's heart swelled with pride and his eyes filled up with tears as he tried to comprehend the enormity of Ian's accomplishment: his son taking part in the national championship. Unfortunately Ian's news only tempered the events of the day back home. Just when Ian thought life could not possibly get any better his father broke the bad news to him.

"It's your Mom Ian, she's taken a turn for the worse." Marie's uterine cancer had been in remission for more than a year, lulling everyone into believing there was much more time.

"I'm coming right home," said Ian, realizing for a moment the sudden unimportance of the day's accomplishments.

"There will be none of that. Your mother will want you to stay and compete. There's nothing you can do for her here."

"But Dad."

"No, stay and win that championship, son, show the world your skills. That's what you can do."

Ian passed on his love to his mother, who was sleeping, and hung up the phone. With a heavy heart and a tearful eye, he explained to Stuart his mom's condition. For the first time in forty-eight hours, his mind was not focused on golf. Ian had always put family ahead of everything else. As he told Stuart that his father insisted he stay, Stuart could see the emotional turmoil in Ian's eyes.

"Your father's right Ian, your mother would want you to compete. They must both be so proud of you." Stuart told Ian he must focus all his thoughts on the championship. This was easier said than done. Ian did not sleep that evening, not because of golf, but because of the enormous conflict his conscience was providing.

CHAPTER EIGHTEEN

The following morning Stuart and Ian arrived at Troon and made their way to the player's locker room for the first of several practice rounds. People were convinced that Stuart was the player and Ian his caddy, but as word spread of Ian's accomplishments at the qualifier a number of players introduced themselves and expressed their congratulations.

Arnold Palmer, the great American, in a wonderful gesture of kindness congratulated Ian and invited him along for a practice round that day.

Ian was practically speechless, "It would be an honor sir."

"Call me Arnie," said Palmer, "Oh and do you mind if Gary Player joins us?"

"Why yes, I mean no, of course that would be great," stammered Ian. Ian thought he was out of his league. It's not too late to go home he thought. Stuart would have nothing to do with that, besides he wanted to meet Palmer and Player and see them play up close.

Pleasantries were exchanged and Ian was given honors on the first tee. A small gallery by Monday's standards of about one hundred had gathered to watch these two legends and this unknown lad show their stuff.

Stuart was as excited as Ian as they assembled at the first tee. "Remember to focus, oh yeah and let's have fun." But the thought of his mother, his playing partners, the gallery and the overall enormity of the upcoming week were too much for young Ian. He proceeded to shank his tee shot into the high grass of an adjacent fairway.

"That's perfectly fine Ian," said Palmer, "I remember doing that the first time I played with Gene Sarazen. Tee up another and we'll write that one off to nerves." These words of reassurance settled Ian's nerves and as an enormous calm overtook him he rifled his second drive right down the middle.

Player turned to Palmer, "Well Arnold, it looks like we've got our work cut out for us." Hole after hole Ian demonstrated a strategy and mastery of the elements that Robert and William had promised would hold up on any course. Palmer and Player had great talent, and while the round was meant to gain familiarity with the course, the green speeds, breaks and possible hole locations both men were now fully aware of whom the competition would be that week.

It didn't take long following that day's practice round before talk whirled about the locker room. The name Ian McCoren was on the tongue of every player. No one knew him, no one had heard of him before this week, but here he was on the eve of the greatest test of golf as the player everyone was gunning for.

"Nerves," said someone, "That'll do him in. He may have the game for a qualifier or before a few onlookers but when he sees the size of the galleries this week he'll fold like a cheap suit."

"I'll bet he doesn't make the cut," said another whose mouth was considerably larger than his talent.

In the U.K. betting on sporting events was not only legal, it was a form of sporting event unto itself. Now that Ian had made The Open Championship, Stuart decided he would show his confidence in his friend's son. Without telling Ian, Stuart placed a two hundred pound wager on him to win. Since no one had ever heard of Ian, the odds were established at 250 to 1. Throughout the day on Wednesday word had spread of Ian's talents and the odds makers began to hedge their odds downward. Just prior to the first tee shot being hit, Ian's odds of winning, at least in the eyes of those taking bets had dropped to 150 to 1.

CHAPTER NINETEEN

Well, dawn broke on Thursday and Stuart found Ian again fully dressed and sitting on the end of his bed.

"Relax," said Stuart, "You don't go off until one o'clock." After a less than leisurely breakfast of eggs and toast Ian paced anxiously about the house staring miles away.

"This is killing me Stuart. Can we head over to the course now?"

"You bet son, said Stuart, maybe hitting a few balls will help you relax." Ian and Stuart arrived at the course four hours ahead of their starting time, but now Ian could at least breathe.

My luck was about to take a turn for the better. By way of introduction, my name is Trevor O'Garn and at the time I was a spry forty-six year old caddie at Troon. My formal education ended at age eleven when I proved to my father that I could finally carry a golf bag for eighteen holes. From that day I began a new education of sorts. My life education, the one that helped men pay the bills, came up and down the swales and hillocks of my home course, Troon. Though I had never traveled more than a few miles from my birthplace, I had the opportunity, through conversation and just listening, to learn of lands far and wide. I felt as though I had been to England, Ireland and even the United States. Some would say there wasn't a blade of grass that grew along the fairways of Troon that didn't have my permission. While there were quirky bounces and an occasional twist of fate that would send an ordinarily great shot into the depths of a menacing sod faced bunker, I felt as though I knew every square inch of my Troon.

That day I arrived at 6:30 to prepare for my loop. I readied my apron and got a draft of the hole locations. With a little more than an hour to go before our scheduled tee time, I sensed something was not right. Peter Thomson, five-time Open Champion and my boss for the week, had not yet arrived. I placed a call to the house where he was a guest for the duration of the tournament, but there was no answer. As I arrived at the registration desk at the entrance of the clubhouse I spotted him. He was hunched over and had all he could do to lift his head and apologize to me.

"Trevor," he said, "I'm terribly sorry but I have just withdrawn from the event. Through the night something has happened and I find myself in excruciating pain. I feel as though I've let you down." Thomson reached into his pocket and passed me fifty pounds for the practice rounds and my inconvenience. "I hope this is enough. I'm sorry, perhaps you can find another bag." Though this was a sizeable wage for two qualifying rounds and a practice round, I was expecting three more days of work. My emotions were mixed as I felt badly about his back, but all the same I needed the money. Another bag I thought, the competition had already begun. Players were on the course, at the range or on their way.

"Perhaps another caddie slept in a bed like yours Mr. Thomson," I said, "If not, it looks dim."

As I walked out of the entrance toward the putting area, I spotted him, a face so fresh, so young, striding towards me.

"Ian," yelled Stuart, "This way." Ian McCoren, I thought to myself, I had heard talk of him earlier that week. Some of the other veteran caddies had mentioned him all too often throughout the morning. Some of the caddies had even gone as far as to place wagers on him. At 150 to 1, a five-pound bet would pay more than a month or more of loops.

This, of course, was my opportunity. I walked over to Stuart and Ian and introduced myself.

"Pleasure to make your acquaintance," I said, "My name is Trevor O'Garn."

"Ian McCoren," the lad replied, "A pleasure to meet you sir."

"It's a pleasure to finally meet you Trevor." said Stuart, "You're a bit of a legend around these parts. I've heard there's not a man alive who knows this course better than you." I nodded appreciatively knowing perhaps Stuart was right.

"Aren't you're on Peter Thomson's bag this week Trevor?" questioned Suart. "I saw you with him on one of the practice rounds."

"Until about ten minutes ago I was working for Mr. Thomson." I said. Ian was very familiar with the name and both his accomplishments and reputation.

"You WERE?" said Stuart, "What happened?"

"He just withdrew from the event with a bad back," I said, "So technically I'm unemployed."

Stuart took very little time to assess the situation and in a moment of opportunistic greed asked me if I might take his place on Ian's bag for the tournament. Ian looked at Stuart quizzically, uncertain as to the ramifications of this inquiry. Fate had presented Stuart, Ian and myself with opportunities serving each of us in different ways. I was about to leave the ranks of the unemployed, Ian was about to get a caddy who had walked these fairways since before he was born, and Stuart was about to become a spectator whose wager was now looking even more promising.

Stuart turned to Ian and said, "Ian, you might win this tournament with me on your bag, but with Trevor on your bag you will win it." A stout handshake and Stuart passed Ian's bag over to me.

"The gods themselves hand crafted these sticks lad. I recognize the maker. How did you get a set of Old Tom Morris's?" Ian explained his great-grandfather's friendship and the legacy of the clubs. I was spellbound.

"Let them have their bloody technology lad," I said, "These have a heart and soul of their very own".

"I'll be watching you the whole way Ian," said Stuart, "Good luck." Stuart stood aside as Ian and I got to know each other.

"I can tell a great deal about a man by his swing and his clubs. It's going to be an absolute treat to work with you these next three days."

"Well two days anyway," said Ian.

"There'll be none of that negative thinking around me lad. It's just a matter of making sure they spell your name right on that jug."

Ian and I made our way to the range to resume our assessment of each other.

"Start low son and let me see you hit this mashie." I said very little as Ian hit one club after another. When he had made his way through the entire bag he looked at me and said, "Is everything okay Trevor?"

"More that okay lad, it's perfect. This afternoon the wind will freshen and you're going to have to shape your shots and keep them low." Without any noticeable adjustment, Ian punched out a low draw, a knock down, a fade that failed to rise above my nose and an assortment of other shots that brought the broadest of smiles to my wrinkled wind swept face. I wondered to myself how someone so young could have developed such a variety of shots.

"Leave some in the bag. And let's see a few putts. They're going to be faster than they have been all week. And if we don't get any rain by Saturday, this Open will be won with this club," I said, as I marveled at Ian's putter. Like the other clubs this too was crafted by hand of rams horn and brass with a fruitwood shaft and leather wrap. It had a soul, a breath, a heartbeat. This was the key to the Championship.

I excused myself for a few minutes as Ian and Stuart grabbed a bite to eat. I grabbed a sandwich and a wee nip shortly before we headed to the first tee.

"Well lad," I said, "It all starts somewhere. These people are not here to see you fail, now don't disappoint them."

Ian nodded appreciatively as he was introduced. His playing

partner that day would be the very gracious and talented Kel Nagle. The galleries following the marquee players were still on the course but a number of spectators had made the first tee their home for the day. Ian had expected to see a large gallery but he seemed totally unprepared for this.

"Relax son," I said, "Pretend you're home playing a quick round with your Dad." This comment had brought out a flood of emotions about the accident, his father, his mother and I sensed I had said something wrong.

"I'm sorry son. You do play with your Dad?" Ian began to explain about his dad's accident, his mother's sickness and as tears filled up his eyes I knew I had to do or say something to get him to refocus.

I stood an inch or so from Ian's face and staring him straight in the eyes I whispered, "We must focus Ian if we are to be successful today. Twenty seconds is all I ask for on the first tee. Shut out the world and send that ball down the right half of the fairway." I handed Ian his spoon and as our eyes met I gave him a reassuring nod and stepped back. Ian could feel his own heart pounding in his chest as he looked down at the ball. He drew a deep breath and as he released it he took back his club and gracefully and effortlessly sent the ball on the route I had described. A slight breeze blew in from the water and set his ball to rest in the center of the fairway. As it rolled to a stop, a thunderous roar, the first of many we would hear that day, echoed through the once still air. With the tee shot behind us my job was to keep Ian calm and focused. Caddying was so second nature to me that I assumed my new role of psychiatrist.

"There's a bit of a wind off the water so why don't you take it to the right of that front bunker," I said, "Land the ball there with a taste of fade and it will release back to the hole." I felt as though all I had to do was say so and my request would be fulfilled. The ball bounced left and scooted back to within a foot of the hole.

"Don't look so surprised lad. Just do as I say and let's have ourselves some fun today." I was energized and found a vigor that these old bones had not seen in years.

"Deep breath lad," I said as I passed him his putter. Ian wasted little time as he sank his first birdie of The Open Championship. The second hole was a bit longer and bunkers skirted the edge of the fairway. The wind was freshening and so I handed Ian his spoon again.

"Take this one down the right edge of the fairway lad, Mother Nature will take care of the rest." His tee ball had again found the center of the fairway and he had but a short iron to the green.

"The right bunker is again the target," I said, as I passed him his niblick. Ian's ball danced and settled about six paces to the left of a pin cut just two paces from the right edge. A two put par followed as well as a sense of calm for both Ian and myself. Three again was cut from the same fabric as one and two and Ian executed another par. Four is a challenging par five with an angled fairway.

"Take this to the right of the flag son," I said, "And don't hold back." His tee shot sailed high into the sky and afforded Nagle an opportunity to see Ian's driver in action.

"You should have no problem getting there in two," I said, as I reached for his driver and we watched Nagle tee off. Nagle must have felt some sense of urgency as he took a very aggressive line to the pin. His ball hung out to the right and he was forced to chip back to the fairway with a lay up. Ian had only two hundred and forty-one yards to the pin and the wind was fresh and over my right shoulder.

I handed Ian his spoon, "Take this to the tee box on number five and get it up in the air." Ian executed the shot to perfection and the ball landed ever so softly and trickled to the back edge of the green some two or three paces from the pin. Nagle's approach was stiff and he tapped in for birdie.

"Great shot!" said Ian, as he and Nagle headed for the green. Ian looked at his putt a number of times before turning to me and saying, "I don't see anything."

"Then the center of the cup it is." Ian's putt was straight to the hole and his eagle got him to three under after four. The roars echoed down the fairway and drew spectators like bees to honey.

Hole number five was a lengthy par three of 210 yards with four bunkers left and in front and a stretch of beach to the right. The wind was off the water and the tiny green brought these bunkers into play.

"Take it at the right edge with a wee bit of fade," I said. I handed Ian his spoon and for just a second he looked at me as if it were too much club for the distance.

"I know you're full of juice right now lad, but hit this one as smooth as ten year old scotch."

The ball headed out to sea and, with nature's help, retuned to the back fringe for a two-putt par. Given the damage this hole would provide that day, a three was a great score.

Mr. Nagle was one under at this point but by the look on his face you would think it was much worse.

Number six was an even longer par five than number four with bunkers guarding the left and right of the landing area. This was the last par five on the front but clearly not an eagle hole.

"Play this one safely lad, it's near impossible to get there in two." Ian split the fairway with a wonderful drive. As we approached his ball I sensed a bit of hesitation on his part hoping I would give him the go ahead. I pulled his mashie and told him that the right center was a good a line as any. Again, just point and shoot. This was becoming as much fun for me as it was for the gallery. His third shot was a niblick that he put right over the pin. I thought for a moment it was going in. I passed him his putter as we strode to the green, exchanging birdies with Nagle.

On number seven, the wind was a bit at our back off the water. Two bunkers pinch the fairway where the average tee shot would land.

"Take this over the right bunker and show me a wee bit of power."

Ian hit an explosive drive but the wind died and the ball caught the front lip of the right bunker. The crowd let out a slight moan but Ian seemed undeterred. He had all he could do to hit it sideways back to the fairway.

As I set his bag down I turned to him and said, "I'm not worried, are you?" I handed him his mashie again. Nagle had split the fairway short of the bunkers and was on the green in two. Ian strode to the ball, pausing only momentarily, and in a manner befitting someone playing a practice round pinched the ball off the short turf and sent it toward the green. The ball hopped twice and checked up a few inches from the pin.

"I'm not worried," he said as a broad smile covered his face, "Are you?" Here we were at The Open, embroiled in a sea of tension and anxiety, and this lad was having a ball. We walked to the green with a kick in our step and traded pars with an all too unhappy Nagle.

Number eight at Troon is known as the "Postage Stamp". It's a short par three of 126 yards. Innocent enough, but the green is encircled with bunkers and a steep embankment guards the lift side. Just twelve years earlier, German amateur Herman Tissies one putted for a fifteen. Standing on the tee protected from the wind, but turning back into it for the first time, the tendency is to hit too much club. I passed him his niblick and pointed out the target. It was the second time he gave me that look of uncertainty. But his faith was unwavering and he struck the ball perfectly. A roar from the crowd let us know he had pulled off the shot.

"It nearly went in!" an onlooker said as we reached the green. A birdie putt and we were back on track. Nagle changed clubs after Ian's tee ball but two putted to fall further back.

Nine, the longest par four on the front side was our last chance to have a helping wind. The remaining holes were nearly all dead into the wind that was stiffening in the late afternoon. The hills to the right are menacing, so too are the bunkers that guard the outside of the dogleg. I gave Ian his spoon and told him to aim at the bunkers. His ball landed short of the bunkers leaving him a lengthy second shot.

It was, however, from the fairway. Nagle took a more aggressive line and his ball was headed for the gorse when the wind brought it back toward the fairway. It settled in the rough but was some forty yards ahead of Ian.

"Play your ball," I warned, "This isn't match play." I passed him his jigger and told him not to let the ball get above his shoulders. He executed the shot perfectly and the ball ran and ran like a scared rabbit to the front of the green. Nagle hit a short iron with an abbreviated follow through. It skirted the green but settled only feet from the pin. His birdie putt would lift his spirits as we made the turn. As they headed to the back nine, Nagle was three under but trailing someone he never heard of before by two strokes.

The back nine at Troon is where the men are separated from the boys. It plays into the wind in one direction or another forcing players to hit shots that are not usually in their bags. Number ten was a lengthy par four by 1962 standards with a blind tee shot. The wind was going to make it play like a par five that day.

"Take this ball as far left as that hillock," I said as I passed Ian his driver. Nagle had been a bit conservative with his tee ball and I wondered if he would reach the green in two. Ian hit a terrific drive that fought the wind and ran down the fairway some 100 yards ahead of Nagle. The elation Nagle exhibited following the birdie on nine was quickly disappearing. His three-wood got up in the air and the wind slapped it back to earth some thirty yards short of the green. Nagle was no doubt wondering what the afternoon held in store for him.

"Let's show off a bit," I said to Ian as I passed him his mashie.

"Hit a low runner like I know you can and let see if we can't scare the cup."

Ian's command of golf shots was so remarkable that I wondered if there was any shot he was incapable of pulling off. And so with little noticeable adjustment in his stance he sent the ball down the right side of the fairway. It turned back to center and scrambled back just below the pin.

"Like that?" he said, with a wry smirk only I could appreciate. Most would take his comment as arrogance but my brief courtship with the lad led me to believe that each of us had found a new friend to enjoy The Open with.

"Let me know when you're having fun?" I said, as I passed him his putter. Nagle chipped to the green but his ball released to the back and his stroke on nine was given back with a two-putt bogey. Ian's birdie resulted in a two shot swing. Nagle now found himself four shots back. As the gallery began to grow, so did the curiosity regarding the course record.

The back nine plays to a par 36 with two par fives. But the wind which was now gusting to two and sometimes three clubs made it feel as though there were seven par fives and two threes.

Eleven was by today's standards a par four, but this 463-yard par five hole was sheer terror. The railway ran down the right side of the hole and was out of bounds. Trouble down the left side made it an equally poor alternative. Ian hit a wonderful drive but was left with nearly the same distance to the pin. I could tell he wanted to hit driver off the deck but it was time to harness the exuberance of youth and play a bloody old man's game. I gave Ian his cleek, which would be the weapon of choice for the remainder of the day. "It may not get you there, but I don't want to have to lift my eyes to watch the flight of your next shot." Ian's shot started out low and scampered up just short of the green. A delicate chip and two putts for par gave us both a sense of what lied ahead.

Twelve was a bit of a respite as we headed back toward the water. A dogleg left with a right to left wind, an aggressive tee shot would shorten this hole considerably. Ian shaped a spoon and let the wind guide his ball down the fairway. His second shot was a mashie from one hundred and eighty five yards.

"Take this one out over the right bunker and the wind will do the rest," I said. Ian had managed another two-putt par and an opportunity to catch our breath, if only for a second.

"No rest for the weary," I said as we reached thirteen, a bunkerless 465 yard par four right into the teeth of the wind.

"Tee it down and let it run." Just as he had done on eleven Ian kept the ball on the ground and under the menacing wind. A two-putt par and a huge sigh of relief was our reward as headed to the next hole.

Fourteen is a well protected 179 yard par three with two bunkers short right and a back left bunker waiting to gobble up an aggressive tee shot.

I passed Ian his mashie, "Keep you tee shot under control. Let me see a slight draw over that front right bunker, and just over it lad, don't get too carried away!" It wasn't until the ball landed that we both exhaled. It seemed to hang over the bunker forever. When the ball landed it scooted to the back left but fifteen foot past the pin.

I cleaned Ian's ball and handed it to him, "Just breathe on it," I warned, "The wind will do the rest." A sense of commitment to every syllable I uttered was a refreshing change from the know-it-alls, amateur and pros alike, that I had suffered with over the years. The ball just brushed the right edge of the cup and another par was on our card. Nagle had made only pars after his bogey on ten and wasn't gaining any ground.

Fifteen is another lengthy par four bounded on the right by a road, pinched at the landing area and guarded in front by inhospitable bunkers. I gave Ian his driver and told him to keep it low and out to the right. This was an aggressive route but it shortened the hole somewhat and into the wind it was necessary. His tee ball was excellent but he was still left with 203 yards to the green. His cleek was again put into service.

"Carry that front right bunker, mind you, and hug the right side of the green." A deep bunker guards the left side of the green and a blast from it would flirt with the road. Ian's second shot was a thing of beauty as it cleared the bunker some thirty five yards short of the green and raced back to just two feet past the cup. I'm sure everyone was thinking birdie when we reached the green but the wind was whipping Ian's pant legs and he had trouble even placing the ball after I cleaned it.

"Just get it going," I warned, "And trust your line." The ball rolled over the cup as if it weren't even there. The good news was that we had an uphill putt for par. The bad news was that it was from six feet. Ian was determined and not at all dismissed by his first effort. He walked around and without much expression drained the par putt in the center of the cup.

The sixteenth was a 542-yard par five that was playing more like a par seven that day.

"Keep the ball on the ground the whole way and we'll be just fine." Ian hit his cleek three times weaving through the landscape and after two putts a par was his. Nagle took an aerial approach off the tee and the wind knocked his shot some thirty-five yards shy of Ian's cleek. He learned from the youngster that he thought would be his disciple that day and finished the hole on the ground for a matching par.

At 223 yards into the wind, the seventeenth was playing more like a short par four. Two bunkers along the left and three guarding the right made left a slightly better alternative.

"There's a trough up the middle," I said, "Run this cleek up there and don't let the ball get above your waist." I've never had more fun guiding a player around so difficult a course as I did that day. We finally got our second birdie of the back nine as Ian's tee ball nearly went in for the ace. The gallery was delirious as Nagle came to the tee. Nagle's tee ball found the left hand bunker and the gallery, ever appreciative of fine play, applauded his up and down for par.

As we approached the eighteenth tee I warned Ian not to relax quite yet.

"Guide the ball down the middle and mind the bunkers." Ian again did just as I requested and his spoon settled just shy of the fairway bunker leaving him a cleek to this 451 yard final hole. Yet another two-putt par and an enormous sigh of relief brought an end to the most exciting and both physically and emotionally draining round of golf I've had the pleasure to experience. Though Nagle was disappointed to be six shots back, his seventy-one had put him in good standing after one round. He found himself tied with Arnold Palmer just four shots back of some of the players fortunate enough to play early before the winds kicked up. He congratulated Ian and remarked how impressed he was with his ball control. Ian in a most humble and gracious manner passed along all the praise to me.

"I couldn't have done it without Trevor." he said. It's a simple rule of life that caddies are blamed for all the player's shortcomings and the player generally takes the credit for everything else. I was so taken by this young lad that for the first time in my life I found myself speechless.

"Well best of luck." I broke the silence as we exchanged handshakes and headed to the scorer's table. As I gathered Ian's kit, Stuart embraced him with a big hug.

"Well done, Ian," said Stuart, his eyes moist with pride.

"Thanks, that was so much fun."

Ian was exhausted but at the same time infused with excitement as he learned that he was the leader after one round.

"Don't get ahead of yourself lad. The wind could change and bring the field back to us tomorrow." Some players scoffed at this unknown's performance but Palmer, Player and others who witnessed his practice rounds congratulated him and knew there was work to be done.

"Join us for dinner Trevor?" asked Stuart, as he and Ian gathered their things.

"I appreciate it Stuart, but as young as this lad made me feel today, I'll feel that much older if I don't get a warm bath, a wee nip and a fair amount of rest tonight. I'll see you bright and early." As was the case a player who teed off in the afternoon was given an early tee time on day two.

"Besides," I said, "It'll be hours before you leave." Stuart and Ian weren't sure what I meant but, after interview upon interview, they got a quick education about the downside of Ian's accomplishment and his instant celebrity. It was dark when Stuart and Ian arrived at Stuart's house but Ian wanted to phone home and share the highlights with parents. Robert was beside himself with excitement as he and the entire island listened to the action on BBC radio. Emotionally spent from the day's activities and his ongoing concern for Marie, Robert was running on fumes.

"How's Mom?" asked Ian, his heart and his thoughts resting entirely with her.

"She's doing much better," said Robert, "Every birdie lifts her spirits even more."

"If only I knew that, I would have made eighteen of them." Ian's dad let out a great bellow; it was a relief to laugh for a change. Ian and his father replayed every shot and Stuart listened intently with a grin from ear to ear.

"How did you manage to get yourself a professional caddie?" asked Robert.

"I had to pull some strings," said Ian in jest, "Actually, fate took over in that category." Ian proceeded to explain the great fortune they received at the expense of Peter Thomson's back. Ian got his Mom on the line and his smile contradicted the grave look of concern in his eyes. Marie made every effort to disguise her pain as she and Ian spoke.

"Mom, how are you? I can't stop thinking of you."

"I'm doing just fine dear," she said in an ebullient manner as she winced from the incessant pain. "Your playing well is the best tonic I could ever ask for." Ian was momentarily assured by his mother's voice and positive attitude when Robert stepped in to resume the conversation before she could no longer continue her ruse.

"Good luck tomorrow son," said Marie "I love you very much!"

"Bye Mom, love you too," said Ian as his father took back the phone.

"Your mother is quite tired son, in fact we're all a bit exhausted. If your mother and I get some rest we'll be fresh when we listen to your play tomorrow morning." After a brief exchange of "I love you's" Ian put down the phone.

Ian's face was etched with anguish as he turned to Stuart.

"I wish I could be with her."

"There's nothing you can do for her here Ian," said Stuart, "Your playing well is what means the world to her."

The two had an enjoyable, albeit brief, bachelor dinner of leftovers punctuated by recollections of the day's events and optimistic predictions for the morning ahead.

CHAPTER TWENTY

D awn spread her fingers of sunlight over the Ayshire coastline the following morning and an eerie calm permeated the air. Sleep came easily for Ian that evening and dawn arrived all too soon.

Stuart popped his head in at 5:00 A.M. "Ian, it's time," he said, in a voice just above a whisper. Ian sprang to his feet bursting with youthful exuberance. A quick shower and shave followed by toast and eggs and Ian and Stuart were on their way to the club. I was waiting for Ian to arrive.

"Great day lad," I said, "Clear skies and a calm wind. If we were sailing I'd be disappointed, but it's golf we're here for so let's have at it." More handshakes and congratulations met Ian at the range and with a sense of purpose we made our way from the putting green to the first tee. Great applause and a significant gallery met us at the first tee.

Ian turned to me and said, "Let's see if we can't make the cut."

"Let's see if we can't just make a little history instead," I countered. "Do as I say and we're going to turn a few heads today." As much as I enjoyed the first round with this talented young lad, the second round was even more impressive. The first round was a test of will power and concentration against the elements. The second round was a pure exhibition of raw talent. Ian's skills and strategy were a thing of beauty. Not two holes into the back nine and we were already six under par.

The record of seven under 65, that Ian had tied, had stood the test of time. It was about to be changed.

"Don't relax," I said, "Let's put a big dent in that record book." We remained at six under par and finished round two with a thirty-six-hole total of one thirty one. We had a commanding eight shot lead over Tony Jacklin and Arnold Palmer who found the morning weather agreeable as well. Just as it had the day before, the afternoon winds proved to be the undoing for many lads that day. The cut came at three over par and a number of talented but disappointed golfers made their way home a little earlier than they had hoped for.

I turned to Ian and said, "Well, the final pairing on Saturday, this is a great feat." Ian was both ecstatic and yet at the same time distracted. His thoughts were with his mother back home.

"How I wish Mom and Dad could be here to share this day and weekend with me Trevor," he said.

"You're in their thoughts and they're in yours," I reassured him.

Radio broadcast the events of the day and no doubt great cheers were bellowing from the tavern down the road from Ian's home. Robert's friends visited the house shortly after the morning round with dinner and well wishes for Marie. Her spirits were buoyed by the broadcast but the pain from the spreading cancer was a constant reminder of the dire nature of her condition.

"Robert," Marie said, "I don't believe I've ever been more proud in my life. Our son in the final day of The Open Championship."

"I've never even dreamed this could happen." Marie's smile was abbreviated by a stabbing wince as he squeezed her outstretched hand.

"I wish the pain would end Robert, I've been through too much." Robert felt more helpless than ever. His selfish side didn't want to let Marie go but he hated to see her suffer. He would have traded places in an instant rather than see her this way. The doctor was summoned to the house that evening.

"This will help ease the pain," he said, as he gave her an injection of morphine.

"Please don't put me out doctor," Marie pleaded, "I want to hear my son play." Everyone on the small island was well aware of both Ian's accomplishments and Marie's condition. Their hopes and prayers were that Marie would be able to share in Ian's anticipated triumph.

Back at Troon, Ian handled the endless stream of interviews like a veteran. From time to time, a question caused him to think of home, his voice cracked, and his eyes welled up. Stuart stepped in and excused Ian from the group of curious reporters.

"If we stay any longer," Stuart said, "We'll have to go right to the first tee from here." The press laughed at the apparent truth of his comment and thanked Ian for his time. They wished him well on Saturday and one asked for a prediction.

"I bet I'll have eggs and toast tomorrow," Ian fired back, and the group erupted in applause. Ian, Stuart and I had a brief celebration at the tavern then they repaired to Stuart's house as the crowds followed him relentlessly.

"Celebrity," said Stuart, "Is often more difficult to handle than the game itself."

"Me a celebrity, I'm just a golfer."

"Just a golfer, no Ian you're the co-record holder at Troon, the leader after thirty-six holes of The Open Championship and the purist golfer I've ever had the pleasure to see." Jones, Hogan, Nelson, thought Ian, now they were pure golfers.

"But don't let your head get too big lad," warned Stuart, "We're only half way there."

This had become the story of the century, an unknown with skills the likes of which few had ever seen holding the lead in the Open Championship. Ian called home that night and inquired first about his mother's condition.

"The better you play, the better she feels," said his Dad, in and effort to reassure his son that his presence at Troon was the right decision. Her spirits are lifted and her pain has subsided. Hang on son, here she is."

"Ian, I'm so very proud of you."

"Mom, how are you?" Ian asked, "I can't stop thinking of you."

Marie took a deep breath to conceal her anguish, "Ian, I'm doing fine, the pain is much better." Marie did not want to burden Ian with the truth and take away from his remarkable accomplishments that had brought her such pride.

"Pride is the best medicine a mother could ask for Ian. I couldn't be more delighted with you and your performance today. Do your best and have fun, I love you dear."

"Here's your father," she said as she passed the phone to Robert.

"I love you Mom and I'll see you in a few days." Ian hurried to get the words out.

"Now son," said Robert, "The mental side of your game will be your greatest asset tomorrow." You'll feel and incredible amount of pressure. Channel it and use it to your advantage." William and Robert had spent many hours of Ian's youth working outside the swing. The mental toughness they instilled would be of paramount importance over the next two rounds.

"Son, I'm very proud of you," said Robert, "No matter what the outcome."

"I'll do my best."

"We can ask for no more." There was a pause and Ian thanked his father for all he had done.

"I love you son. Play well."

"I love you too, I'll talk to you tomorrow."

Ian lay in bed that evening as childhood memories flooded his head. He had thoughts of his Mom, his Dad and Grandfather of course. He remembered the lessons on the golf course, the successes and failures, and he fell off to sleep with a wry grin on his face.

CHAPTER TWENTY-ONE

Dawn came quickly. It was perhaps the first good night sleep that Ian had since leaving home. His staple of eggs and toast was enjoyed with a combination of enthusiasm and trepidation as he and Stuart were looking forward to the final day at Troon. The day started early and never let up. As soon as breakfast was finished, Stuart went to start the car, but it wouldn't start.

"I must have left the lights on last night," said Stuart, as Ian paced anxiously, "We'll take my other car." Stuart's other car was a small two-seater which he kept in the garage most of the year. He took it out for rides about the countryside, but it had been a while since it had seen the light of day.

"If it starts we're in luck," said Stuart. "If," thought Ian, this was a possibility he did not wish to explore. Stuart turned the key and the engine cranked, and cranked and cranked some more. Just when Ian felt his world was falling in around him the engine turned, a puff of white smoke billowed from the tail pipe and a collective sigh exited both of their mouths. Stuart retrieved Ian's clubs from his wagon and brought them around to the entrance of the garage.

"Let me put this tarp out of the way," said Stuart, as he made a few quick folds in the dusty car cover. There was barely enough space in the garage for the car, let alone two grown men, so Ian waited in the driveway. Ian stared down in total disbelief as Stuart's car backed out and his clubs tipped over from the spot where Stuart had left them.

"No!" Ian's mind screamed out but he was powerless to speak. The clubs fell directly in line with the back right tire. Unable to see them, and with the noise from the engine echoing in the small garage, Stuart put the car in reverse and gunned the engine. As he released the clutch, the car backed over the clubs and the sound of breaking shafts filled the morning air like a stab in the heart to Ian.

The car lifted up momentarily before dropping on the other side of the bag. Stuart looked back to see the void stare in Ian's eyes. He leapt from the car, knowing all too well what had happened. "Ian, I'm so terribly sorry." Ian's hopes were dashed. His chances at The Open Championship were all but over without his clubs. "Perhaps they can be salvaged," he thought, but every shaft was broken.

Stuart pulled some of the clubs from the bag. The shafts were splintered or severed completely.

"Ian you'll have to use my clubs and I'll get these fixed as quickly as possible." Fixed, thought Ian, these clubs were hand crafted; they cannot just be taped or glued. Stuart scrambled to get his clubs out and presented them to Ian.

"Your game will carry you Ian, just do your best." Stuart set the damaged clubs along side his garage and he and Ian headed for the course.

I could tell something was wrong as a tiny little car with two large men and a set of metal-shafted clubs pulled up.

"You thinking of joining us today Stuart? It's been a while since I carried two bags before." Ian could hardly speak and they both looked as if someone had died. Stuart explained the disaster that had just befallen them and the need for Ian to get used to the new clubs as quickly as possible.

"Let's get to the range lad. There's little time to waste." I pulled the clubs out of the car and turned to Stuart.

"We only get to use fourteen clubs," I said as I passed him back an extra driver.

"It's no use, said Ian, I can't feel the ball." While Stuart's clubs were of the finest quality Ian felt as if he were playing with oven mitts on.

Ian was distraught, "There's never going to be enough time to get used to them."

"All we can do is our best. Ian you're a fine player no matter what the equipment." Even the putter felt awkward in his hands as he left putt after putt long on the practice green.

"It's much too heavy," said Ian, "And much too late to start looking for a new one."

"All we can do now lad, is hope for the best."

Stuart raced back to gather the clubs and get them repaired. As he pulled around the corner and turned into the driveway his heart sank. The clubs were gone. He threw open the car door grabbing his forehead in disbelief. Stuart's neighbor was out on the lawn and Stuart ran next door to talk to him. He asked if he had seen the clubs or if anyone had stopped by.

"Some old man picked them up shortly after you left," said the neighbor, "I thought you were throwing them out, they didn't look to be in such great shape."

"Did you happen to see which way he went?" asked Stuart, as the anxiety level started to climbed even higher.

"I don't know. He sort of just disappeared." Stuart raced up and down the street looking frantically for anyone strange but it was of no use. He would have to tell Ian about the clubs, but how? Perhaps his clubs would suffice.

Unfortunately, back at the course, the outcome was just the opposite. Ian struggled to get a feel for the new clubs, and while his ability was still there his lead began to slip away. Short, long, left or right, Ian was growing frustrated.

"I'm dying here!" said Ian, as his lead and patience were quickly evaporating.

"Hang in there lad," I said as I struggled to find the right club to hand him. By the eighth hole Ian had squandered four shots of his eight-stroke lead, but a birdie on number nine buoyed his spirits. Palmer began a charge that was characteristic of his swashbuckling persona. Despite the fact that Ian and I were getting more familiar with our new clubs on the back nine, his performance was still not enough. A three over par round and a four under by Palmer left Ian clinging to a scant one-stroke lead with just eighteen holes remaining.

Stuart arrived at the course in time to see Ian recover enough to maintain his one shot lead. Stuart didn't know how to tell Ian about what had happened. Ian wasted little time after signing his card to ask Stuart about the clubs. As Ian left the scorers tent he could see in Stuart's eyes that something was terribly wrong.

"Will they be ready for this afternoon's round?" Ian asked. In 1962 the Open championship was played over three days with a thirty-six hole final day. Not only was this physically exhausting but mentally draining as well. Ian would have to stave off the greatest golfer of his era as well as his trademark charge that had begun that morning.

Stuart looked solemnly at Ian, "I'm sorry Ian."

"Well what did they say?"

"It's worse than that Ian, they're gone."

"Gone, where?" Stuart explained their disappearance to Ian but Ian just stared off into space, contemplating his dashed hopes at the Open and more importantly the meaning of the clubs themselves.

"Stuart, I can finish the Open with your clubs, maybe even shoot a respectable round, but those clubs are three generations old!" Ian tried to explain the value he placed on the clubs his ancestors entrusted him to safeguard. "They're worth more to me than any Claret Jug, we simply must find them!" I told Ian that there would be time for that tomorrow but we had better get to the range and get more comfortable with the new clubs because our afternoon round was in less than an hour.

"I'm sorry, "said Ian, "It's not your fault. If it were not for you I wouldn't even be playing."

"Get to the range," said Stuart, "We've got an Open to win."

CHAPTER TWENTY-TWO

"Ladies and gentlemen, our final pairing of the day," echoed the announcement. "From the United States, Mr. Arnold Palmer." The Scots loved Palmer and his style of play. He respected the tradition of the Open and they, in turn, admired him for that. His tee shot rocketed down the first fairway accompanied by a great roar of appreciation. The applause slowly died down and again the captain stepped up to address the audience. "Ladies and gentlemen," he said with a certain sense of pride, "From Scotland, Mr. Ian McCoren." I had never heard such a warm and boisterous cheer before and I sensed that it lifted young Ian's confidence.

"Well here it goes," he said as I reached for Stuart's driver from the bag.

"Wouldn't you feel more comfortable with these?" said a voice from the gallery. Ian and I spun around and there before us was Ian's grandfather William. Ian's eyes bugged out from his head.

"Ian," said William, "I wasn't about to trust the repair of these clubs to just anyone." William passed us the bag of clubs he had rescued from Stuart's garage just six hours earlier. One by one Ian pulled the clubs from the bag.

"As good as, no better than before." Ian could feel the magic again. I sensed that William had learned more than just the game from his father and Old Tom Morris.

I switched out a few items into Ian's bag and passed him his driver. With a confident and powerful swing he sent his drive down the center of the fairway passing even the tremendous length of Palmer. Ian hugged William and William wished him luck in the round.

"I have all I'll need right here!" he said as he pointed to his refurbished clubs.

William and Stuart walked the first fairway getting reacquainted. William owed Stuart more than an explanation about the clubs; he also had to explain why he wasn't dead. After all, Stuart watched them lower William's coffin into the ground. He had every right to believe it was because William was dead. William explained that he still had a great zest for life after mourning Claire's passing. He felt like a third wheel and didn't just want to wait around to die. He left to join an old friend who had setup a small golf shop near the Prestwick Golf Club. In letters, his friend had told him of the profits to be made from the sale of his handcrafted clubs to tourists. With William's help they would both be busy and successful. William's talents were put to great use in their new endeavor and he shared in the profits of the new partnership. He had planned to return if the business was a failure but when he read of his own passing he didn't know what to do. As the days and weeks passed it became easier to just say nothing. When he saw Ian's name in the local paper he wanted to get in touch right away, but he was worried that it would adversely affect his grandson's chances. Once Ian had made the cut, William felt it was time to say hello and wish him luck. He was there at the house that morning, trying to think of the right words to say, when the clubs were damaged. He scooped them up and, sensing a pressing need, poured his attention into their repair.

Despite his bewilderment and anger at having been deceived, Stuart was more pleased that William's talents were now in Ian's hands.

Palmer's second shot hit short of the green and he was contemplating his next shot as he turned to watch Ian's effort. Ian hit a delightful bump and run that nestled up about two feet from the flag. A swale in the green blocked our view of the outcome but the roar of the crowd gave Ian and I a sense of how close it really was. The Scots are great fans of the game of golf. They don't really take sides but rather they cheer for the performance. Palmer got up and down for the par and the roar from the gallery was incredible as Ian's birdie putt fell to put him up by two.

"There's too much golf ahead of us to gloat laddie," I warned as we headed to the second tee. Just as he had done in the first round Ian's mastery of the game had belied his age. His approach on two was even more spectacular as it nearly fell in for an eagle. A tap in birdie to Palmer's bogie and Ian found himself up by four. Matching pars on three and four set the tone for and exciting fifth. Ian didn't need his putter as his approach fell in for eagle. Palmer looked over, his head turning from left to right, and then just smiled as they headed for the green. He had charged in the past and swallowed up many great golfers over the years, but here he found himself the victim. If he didn't recover, and fast, he'd find himself playing for second. A birdie on the par four sixth and Ian now found himself five under after six holes. At this pace the Open record was in jeopardy. Palmer birdied number seven to take back a stroke but gave it right back with a bogey on number eight. With matching pars on nine we made the turn with a six shot lead with just nine to play. It's an insurmountable lead people began to say. No one had ever come back from being this far behind. Palmer was not one of those sharing this opinion. He hitched his pants and, with an even more focused look of determination, headed to the tenth tee.

"Let's be hungry but conservative lad. A foolish mistake can take away that lead as quickly as it was had." Ian was not as aggressive a player as Palmer yet I felt certain that we would be able to hold on to our lead. Ian's performance had placed an incredible pressure on the rest of the field to perform. They found themselves being shown up by a player that prior to this week they had never heard of.

The very air around Palmer had seemed to change. He nearly left the ground as he sent his tee shot on number ten down the fairway where there were no other pitch marks. A deft pitch and a curling birdie putt and he had carved away one shot of Ian's lead. They traded pars on eleven and twelve and then Palmer birdied thirteen and fourteen to cut the lead to three with just four holes to play. The gallery had swelled to an enormous but respectfully quiet crowd. I wondered if there were even that many people in all of Scotland. Just as they had cheered Ian's accomplishments on the front nine, so too did the gallery react to Palmer's heroics. I had always been proud of my fellow Scots and their sportsmanship but this was truly a glowing example.

"Enough fun and games." I said as we reached the tee on fifteen, "Let's show him why Scotland is the birthplace of golf." Ian caught a hold of his next drive and his second shot hit the crest of a hillock and released to the hole as the crowd erupted.

"Now that's what I had in mind lad!" I said, as I passed him his putter. Palmer's approach left him a thirty-foot putt for birdie. The gallery was dead silent as Palmer's putt tracked toward the hole. The Scott's were being treated to a match of skills that they had not witnessed before nor, I dare say, since. The roar was deafening as Palmer's putt curled into the side of the hole.

"Answer him lad," I said, "And the crowd will carry you to the next tee." Ian's putt curled slightly to the left, but speed was everything.

"Trust the line and take a deep breath." The putt seemed to take forever but with a final revolution it dropped into the cup. The ground actually began to shake as the crowd let out a tremendous roar. Palmer looked a bit amazed that his charge hadn't shaken this youngster.

Robert and William had passed on the most valuable gift aside from the clubs. Mental strength and competitive toughness were about to carry this young man into the history books. A three shot lead with three to go. I could barely contain my excitement. The sixteenth hole was a sea of humanity as people scurried here and there for a glimpse of something they would tell their grandchildren about.

Palmer's drive was fine and I turned to Ian and said, "It's time!"

Ian hit a powerful drive down the right that was drawing back to the fairway when a gust of wind caught it and deposited it in a bunker. The gallery let out a collective sigh.

"It's okay laddie, let's take one shot at a time." Palmer saw the opportunity to pounce again and his four iron released from the front edge and settled twelve feet below the hole. An eagle attempt would have to wait as Ian surveyed his options.

I handed Ian his mashie, "Pitch out and go for it in three, you'll have your par, possible birdie. It's no time for heroics now." Ian had followed every word of advice to this point. This was no time to go out on his own. His pitch just cleared the front edge of the bunker and rambled down the fairway just one hundred and ten yards short of the green. Given the circumstances and pressure it was perhaps the greatest shot of the day. Ian drew a deep breath and hit his approach shot to the green. It bounced just past Palmer's ball but released hard to the back of the putting surface. It was still his turn as he was outside of Palmer's eagle opportunity. The crowd was silent as he drew back his putter.

The roar grew as the ball approached the hole, but a huge sigh was heard as it fell one revolution shy. A tap in par was better than bogey. Palmer had ample opportunity to examine his putt and wasted little time as he addressed the ball. I thought I would lose my hearing as the screams and roars told the world that he had made eagle.

Here I was with a front row seat to a drama the like of which I had never witnessed, before or since. There we stood, one up with two to play. My nerves were frazzled. I was getting too old for this, I thought. Still, I had to let Ian know that we were still in control. Pars were exchanged on the lengthy par three seventeenth when both players, justifiably excited, hit their tee shots to the back of the green and each two putted.

Eighteen, the final hole of this thirty-six-hole drama that just couldn't get more exciting. Palmer split the fairway with an enormous drive. I wondered how that many people could turn on and off that much clamor like a light switch. Ian stood there rather calmly looking down the fairway at Palmer's drive, the clubhouse in the background, and the sea of his fellow Scots surrounding us. If he were at all nervous, I could never tell. He had all the air of someone playing an afternoon round for a pint. I grabbed him firmly by the shoulders, more to hold myself up.

"Three more strokes to history Ian, let's focus." Ian reached into his pocket for a tee as I passed him a ball. He took his customary two practice swings before addressing the ball. The crowd hushed and he stepped away from the ball. He looked back into the gallery and there was William. Their eyes locked and William winked the same wink he had the first time Ian had swung that club. William's eyes housed a certain mystical sparkle.

"You can do this!" he mouthed, and Ian nodded, turned and strode back to his ball. The silence was deafening, broken only by the crack of Ian's driver as it rocketed his ball down the fairway. It headed toward the left bunker and, as if on cue, turned and settled on the fairway a few yards in front of Palmer. The crowds rushed forward as Ian, myself, Palmer and his caddie were swept up in a sea of well wishing enthusiasts anxious to touch a piece of history. We emerged from the gallery as they were marshaled back to let us not only proceed, but breathe as well.

Palmer was first to play. He hit a beautiful iron to the green. It hopped once and released. As if it had eyes, it rolled to the pin stopping only a foot shy of the hole. The roar that echoed down the fairway let those who were blocked from view know that the charge of Palmer had not subsided. Ian stood without emotion, as the cheers seemed to go on forever. Ian was fully aware of his duties and I stood by his side waiting for a cue.

"Let's finish this," he said, as I passed him his mashie and told him the yardage. Silence overtook the crowd again as he drew back his club. The ball took a low trajectory toward the pin, bounced once, but then took an unusual kick to the left. We watched in disbelief as it wandered for what seemed an eternity before coming to rest about ten paces from the hole. As Ian and Palmer reached the green, Palmer hesitated and offered Ian the gallery's applause. Ian deferred to Palmer, as he was respectful of both his accomplishments and immeasurable talent. In a great gesture the strapping Palmer put his arm across Ian's shoulder as they walked up the last fifty yards together. I would bet that Ian's parents and the entire Isle of Arran could hear the cheers without the aid of a radio at that moment.

Palmer asked Ian if he should mark his putt or finish. Ian allowed him to putt out and again the gallery erupted. Palmer, in his swashbuckling style, had closed the insurmountable gap and was now in position for a playoff or potential victory.

Ian stood thirty feet from the hole but it looked more like three hundred. The pressure I felt was now squarely on my shoulders as I read what I hoped would be the final putt of the Championship.

"It's got a bit of borrow from the right," I said, "It will turn left as it falls in." My final words, "falls in", were what I wanted Ian's brain to hold onto as he prepared to putt. Ian had relied on me for all of his reads and I was never more nervous that he didn't double guess me.

Steely nerves, the kind youth are blessed with, allowed him to draw back his putter. Old Tom Morris and William's hands had blessed this instrument that now kissed the ball and sent it on its voyage. It was out to the right the first twenty or so feet. "Turn," I said, as it started to slow down. It was heading to the cup as the crowd began to clamor. "Lord give it enough pace," I begged as it approached its final destination. It stopped at the edge of the cup, its dimples staring into the abyss. The groan from the crowd was like a wave as it spread back through the fairway to those now fifty deep. A par, a playoff, and a chance at the title: all these thoughts raced through my head as I stared at the ball, but go in out shouted them all. Ian paused for a moment in disbelief. Palmer knew he had dodged a huge bullet and the confidence he felt from the recent holes would be a great advantage in the upcoming playoff. He removed his hat as Ian approached what would be an obligatory par.

With just two strides remaining before he reached his ball, a cool breeze, the kind that had been absent all day, made its presence known as it blew briskly across the green. My hat was removed for what was to be a congratulatory handshake with Palmer and the few hairs on my head wavered. Ian was looking at Palmer and I at him when the thunderous roar from the crowd broke the silence. The ball dropped in and the Championship was his. We all stood in utter disbelief, unsure of what to say. The emotions of the day, his life, my life had shot to the surface.

Palmer stood there stoically for a moment or two but ever the gentleman, strode toward Ian with his hand firmly extended. Ian was without words as the two embraced.

"I gave it my best," said Palmer, "But today is your day, relish the moment and congratulations!" Ian's eyes filled with tears. He was not the only one. As I looked about at the ocean of my screaming countrymen my own eyes could not hold back my happiness.

Perhaps the ghost of Old Tom Morris had persuaded the ball to fall, but many to this day believe it was Ian's mother Marie, whose final words, as she passed away at that very moment, were "Go in". A sadness and elation, the likes of which should never share the same stage, filled Ian's home that afternoon. Robert held Marie's hand as tears streamed down his cheeks.

Ian was swept up by the crowd as the engraver went about placing his name and score to the base of the claret jug. I felt like a teenager again. Fate, that a fickle and uncontrollable force, that placed me on the bag of one of golf's greatest dramas.

As the excitement waned Ian turned to me and through tear filled eyes said, "Trevor, I can never thank you enough for all you've done!"

"It is I who should be thanking you lad, this has been the most exciting week of my life!"

Ian turned to Stuart and whispered in his ear. Stuart pulled his wallet from his pocket and handed Ian a fist full of bills.

Ian turned to me and offered me a healthy wage for my efforts.

"There'll be none of that son, remember you're an amateur. Besides I wagered the fifty pounds Peter Thompson gave me on you to win. I'm one rich caddie!"

Ian was unable to receive the prize money because of his amateur status. He did, however, receive the coveted "Claret Jug" and low amateur medal for his accomplishments. With swollen eyes and the broadest if smiles he turned to William and pointed out the first name on the body of the trophy. It was that of great grandfather's friend Tom Morris Jnr.

The celebration continued, as did the countless requests for interview from the various media. Ian asked if he could use a phone to call home.

CHAPTER TWENTY-THREE

A friend of the family had placed himself outside the front door of Robert and Marie's home to inform the scores of well-wishers of Marie's passing. The silence within was broken by the phone's ring. Robert answered in a voice that let Ian know something was wrong.

"Dad it's Ian, is everything okay?"

Robert was speechless, not knowing whether to congratulate his son or break the sad news to him first.

"Is Mom all right, can I talk to her?"

With that Robert began to sob and Ian knew his mother had passed. As Robert sat down the priest reached for the phone. "Ian, it's Father Barnes, your Mom has passed."

The enormous elation Ian was experiencing had vanished instantly. Stuart was nearby, still caught up in the excitement, when he noticed the expressionless stare on Ian's face. He crossed the room as quickly as possible. It was a moment before Ian's attention was captured. He just turned and passed the phone to Stuart as he began to cry.

"Hello, this is Stuart," he said to the priest still on the line.

Father Barnes remembered Stuart from his parish years ago, "Stuart, this is Father Barnes, Marie has passed away."

"May I speak to Robert?"

Robert had regained some composure as he and Stuart exchanged emotions.

Robert was emphatic, "Don't let this rob him of his accomplishment!"

"It's much too late for that, Robert," said Stuart, "You know that family is above all else for Ian."

Stuart knew that Robert needed some time alone to digest all that had happened.

"We'll call back later and we'll see you tomorrow Robert. Again my condolences."

With that Stuart put down the receiver and turned to hug Ian. "Ian, I'm so deeply sorry for your loss. Let's gather your belongings and make our way back to Arran."

As the media rushed toward Ian with more questions, Stuart intervened and informed them of Marie's passing. A silence fell over the crowd and murmurs of condolences spewed forth. William, who had been with me, caught wind of the unsettled air and was informed of his daughter-in-law's passing.

William and Stuart accompanied Ian home for the funeral. William was able to experience something unique when he saw, for the first time, a gravestone bearing his name within the family plot where Marie was laid to rest. Robert and William had a long talk and everything was put behind them. Ian took a lengthy rest from the game over the next few months.

CHAPTER TWENTY-FOUR

In late February of 1963 Ian received and envelope postmarked Augusta, Georgia, USA. He opened the envelope to discover an invitation to play in the Masters Tournament. As he read the invitation, a dull ache permeated his body and he flashed back to the phone call home following his Open victory. Tears streamed down his cheeks as the emotions of that call and the utter helplessness he felt rushed to the surface. A few days later, Ian sent a hand written note to the chairman of Augusta National Golf Club informing him of his regrets to not participate. He thanked them for their invitation but informed them that he was taking a brief rest from the game. Ian finally understood what his grandfather meant when he talked about losing the joy of the game. The very thought of competing in golf, on a major scale, brought about a crushing flood of anxiety.

Ian sent a letter in the same tone to the USGA following his invitation to play in the U.S. Open. Both Robert and William tried, to no avail, to encourage him to play, but the guilt he housed from his absence as his mother passed, had all but vanquished his enthusiasm for the game.

That summer Ian traveled to Royal Lytham and St. Annes to attend the British Open. With a heavy heart he informed the R & A of his intentions to follow in the footsteps of Bobby Jones and retire from the game at his zenith. This news took the golf world by surprise but many believed that, after a period of mourning his mother's passing, Ian would again play competitively.

Ian truly loved the game of golf, but he never again played a round with anything more that a pound or two on the line. The volume of tourists nearly doubled as word spread of the twelve-hole gem where Ian learned to play. William stayed and convinced his friend to help him handle the demand for replica clubs similar to those Ian used to win the Open.

On the mantle of the clubhouse, beneath the golf club of Old Tom Morris, sat a replica of the claret jug. Ian, Robert and William stood there gazing upon the mementos. A one hundred year thread had woven its way through two families, five generations and a singular love for the game of golf.

The children on the island clamored around Ian whenever he was about. Ian told the children to never let go of their "claret dreams".

A little more than two years later, Ian and his childhood sweetheart were married in a small but joyous celebration. Stuart presented Ian with a fifty thousand pound wedding gift. "It was the wager I placed on you to win the Championship," said Stuart.

A year later Ian and his new bride welcomed a daughter into the world. If Robert was not thrilled enough to be a grandfather, he was truly taken when Ian and his wife decided to name their daughter Marie. Twelve year later, Marie was given William's clubs. And so the legacy continues.

GLOSSARY

brassie-a hickory shafted wood with a loft similar to a modern day two-wood.

cleek-a hickory shafted wood with a loft similar to a modern day four-wood.

feathery-a golf ball made by stuffing wetted feathers into a spherical leather housing.

guttie-a golf ball made from the dried sap of the palliquium gutta tree of Malaysia.

jigger-a hickory shafted iron with a loft similar to a modern day four-iron.

mashie-a hickory shafted iron with a loft similar to a modern day five-iron.

niblick-a hickory shafted iron with a loft similar to a modern day nine-iron.

spoon-a hickory shafted wood with a loft similar to a modern day three-wood.

whipping-thread used in wrapping the area of a hickory shafted club where the shaft meets the head.

CPSIA information can be obtained at www.ICGtesting.com
Printed in the USA
LVOW11s0251200415

435276LV00001B/72/P